About the author

David Fuller is an FA-qualif[...]
currently coaches a youth fo[...]
He has worked as a journali[...]
during which time he has written for numerous
publications on a variety of different subjects. David
lives in Newhaven, East Sussex with his wife, two
sons and cat Merry.

Other books by David Fuller

Alfie Jones and a Change of Fortune
Alfie Jones and the Missing Link
Alfie Jones and an Uncertain Future
Alfie Jones and the Big Decision

To Mile Oak Primary

RDF Publishing
3 Courtlands Mews, Church Hill, Newhaven,
East Sussex,
BN9 9LU

Alfie Jones and a test of character
A RDF Publishing book

First published in Great Britain by RDF Publishing in 2012
This version published 2016
Printed and bound in Great Britain by Clays Ltd,
St Ives plc.

3 1 2
Text copyright © David Fuller
Images courtesy of Rob Smyth
(http://www.robsmythart.com)

David Fuller asserts the moral right to
be identified as the author of this work

ISBN 978-0-9570339-1-7

For more exclusive Alfie Jones content, visit:
www.alfie-jones.co.uk

ALFIE JONES AND A TEST OF CHARACTER

DAVID FULLER

**Illustrated by
Rob Smyth**

www.alfie-jones.co.uk

Chapter one

The referee blew his whistle. Alfie Jones took five steps back, not once taking his eyes off the ball on the penalty spot.

This was it. Score here and Alfie knew that Brazil would be guaranteed third place in the Kingsway Summer Soccer School World Cup.

He also knew that a goal would give him a chance of winning the tournament's top scorer award.

Going into the last round of matches, Alfie was one of three players to have scored four goals in the tournament. The other two players were Alfie's best friend, Billy Morris, and Hayden Whitlock, a boy Alfie hardly knew. Billy and Hayden were, at that very moment, playing for

1

opposite sides in the competition's final on a nearby pitch. Alfie didn't know what the score in that match was, though. He'd been far too busy concentrating on his own game.

Alfie slowly moved his head up to look at the goal. He knew exactly where he wanted to put the ball. Into the bottom right hand corner. As close to the post as possible without actually hitting it. "A penalty hit low and hard into the corner is almost impossible for a goalkeeper to save," Alfie's favourite football coach Jimmy Grimshaw had once told him.

He took a deep breath and started his run up. His left foot connected with the ball perfectly. Before the goalkeeper even had a chance to move the ball had found its intended target, much to the penalty taker's obvious delight.

Brazil were now 2-0 up against Holland and with only seconds of the game remaining it was almost certain that the team wearing the bright yellow bibs would finish the Kingsway Summer Soccer School World Cup in third place.

Sure enough, the full-time whistle sounded at the very moment Holland restarted the game. Alfie punched the air with glee, then went to shake hands with the opposition players, most notably Liam Walker, one of Alfie's Kingsway Colts under 9s – soon to be under 10s – teammates.

Playing for the Kingsway Colts on a Sunday morning was Alfie's favourite thing in the whole world, especially since Jimmy Grimshaw had returned as the team's coach following a short illness last Christmas. Although the Colts tended to lose as many games as they won, the quality of football the team played was truly spectacular. "It's just like watching Brazil," Billy's Dad often joked to Billy and Alfie. Just as importantly, though, the whole team always enjoyed playing – even when they lost (although not as much as they did when they won, obviously).

Four Colts players had spent the past week attending the Kingsway Summer Soccer School which ran for five days during the summer holidays; Alfie, Billy, Liam and Chloe Reed.

The World Cup tournament had taken up the majority of the final day, and while it had been enjoyable, the four Colts teammates were only really using the competition as practice for that Sunday's mini-soccer tournament in Ashgate, which their team had entered.

"Well played, Alfie. Good goal," said Liam as he shook Alfie's hand, before quickly adding, "It was never a penalty, though. Your player definitely dived."

Alfie smiled but decided not to get into an argument with Liam about the penalty decision. Liam had already spent most of the game sulking as he had been asked to play in defence. He hated playing in defence – he only ever wanted to play as a striker. Liam simply loved scoring goals – and he scored a lot. He had finished the previous season as the Colts' top scorer with 23 goals, three more than Billy. Alfie, after a slow start, had ended up with five, a total he was fairly happy with but one he would be looking to at least double in the coming season.

"Do you know how Billy and Chloe are getting on in the final?" Alfie asked his friend.

Liam shrugged his shoulders. "I think I saw Argentina celebrating one goal, but I'm not really sure."

The game was still going on so Alfie and Liam wandered over to watch the last few moments of the match. Billy and Chloe did not look happy at all.

Billy was standing on the halfway line with his arms folded, angrily shaking his head from side to side, while Chloe was, unusually for her, moaning at the referee over a decision he had made which she clearly did not agree with.

"What's the score?" Alfie asked a boy who had already been standing watching the game for a minute or so.

"4-0 to Argentina," the boy answered. "That Hayden's scored all four."

This was clearly a shock to Alfie. He, along with most of the other children on the course, had widely expected Spain to easily win the whole tournament. After all, that was the team Billy was playing for, and he had been by far and away the best player at the course all week.

"Wow," said Liam, obviously impressed by what he had just heard. "Billy won't like that at all."

Just as Liam finished uttering his sentence, the referee blew his whistle to signal the end the game. Nearly all of the Argentina players leapt up in the air and bundled on top of each other, taking great delight in their victory. However, one player wasn't celebrating.

Despite the fact that he'd scored all four of his team's goals, Hayden Whitlock had just walked off the pitch without celebrating or even shaking hands with the other team. He was now sitting all by himself in front of the table where some medals and certificates were soon to be given out to the tournament's winners. He wasn't even smiling.

Alfie and Liam ran over to Billy, who was already starting to look a little less angry than he had been while the game was going on.

"What happened, Billy?" both boys asked at the same time.

"He happened. He's amazing," replied Billy, pointing towards the lone figure of Hayden. "Who is he?"

This was a question that neither Alfie nor Liam could answer. Hayden had only turned up to the Soccer School for that final day and hadn't really spoken to anyone, even though a few of the children had made the effort to try and to speak to him.

"How come Hayden only came today?" Liam asked one of the course's coaches as all the boys and girls began to make their way towards the presentation area.

"I think he's only just moved to Kingsway from Norton," the coach answered. "His Mum phoned me last

6

night and asked if it would be alright if he turned up for the day and I said that would be fine. He's a good player isn't he?"

"He's alright, I suppose," replied Liam, trying desperately not to seem too impressed by the new boy.

"Hey, Alf," said Billy, gently nudging his best friend in the back. "Do you think we should ask him to come training with the Colts tomorrow? He'd be well good to have on the team."

Alfie took a moment to think about what Billy was suggesting. Part of him didn't really want any new players to sign for the Colts – especially ones that were better at football than he was. Alfie had spent enough time being a sub when Keith Johnson had been the Colts' coach while Jimmy was ill. He knew that the more players there were in the squad, the more often it would be his turn to miss out on a starting place. At the same time, though, if even Billy was saying that Hayden was a good player then he must be really, really good.

"Yeah, sure," Alfie answered after a short pause. "Let's go and ask him now."

Both boys rushed over to Hayden, who was still sitting all by himself.

"Hi Hayden," said Alfie, cheerfully.

The new boy didn't respond. It was as if he hadn't even heard Alfie speak.

"You played really well in that final," commented Billy. "Some of your skills were brilliant."

"Thanks," replied Hayden, barely loud enough for the two friends to hear him.

Billy and Alfie looked at each other and shrugged their shoulders. Hayden still hadn't even turned to look at them.

"Well..." Alfie ventured, a little unsure about how to continue a conversation with somebody who clearly didn't want to talk. "We were just wondering if you'd like to come and play for our team, the Kingsway Colts? We train every Saturday morning at the Kingsway Recreation Ground. You should come along."

For the first time Hayden lifted his head to look at the two boys who had approached him. "No. I don't think so," he answered, before turning his head back in the direction of the table.

Not sure of what else they could say, Alfie and Billy left Hayden alone and went to sit with Liam and Chloe who were sitting towards the back of the group of children that had gathered near the table.

"What did he say?" asked Chloe.

"Not a lot," replied Alfie.

"Yeah," said Billy. "He's really rude."

Alfie nodded in agreement.

Liam was just about to say something when the chattering children were hushed by the two coaches. They were ready to give out the awards for the course.

Billy, as most of the group had expected, was named player of the week. Equally unsurprisingly, Hayden won the player of the tournament and top scorer awards. While it was obvious to tell from the smile on Billy's face that he was chuffed to have won a medal, it was impossible to see if Hayden was in the slightest bit bothered about his two prizes. He didn't smile once. Not even a little bit.

As they continued to sit listening to the coaches, the four Colts players started to take the mickey out of Hayden behind his back, pulling the most miserable faces they possibly could. Unfortunately, Liam pulled a face so funny that all four children couldn't help but to laugh out loud.

However, as the four friends tried their very hardest to stop themselves from giggling out loud, they were totally unaware that the next time they would see Hayden Whitlock they wouldn't be laughing.

Chapter two

Friday night was usually family film night in the Jones household. Most weeks, Alfie, together with his Mum, Dad and younger sister Megan, would all go down to the local DVD hire shop to choose a film that they all wanted to watch.

This was easier said than done.

The fact of the matter was that each and every week Alfie and Megan failed to agree on anything that they both wanted to watch and after almost ten minutes of bickering it would be left up to Mr or Mrs Jones to pick something. This was more often than not the cue for even more arguing as either Alfie or Megan, sometimes both, then spent a few minutes complaining about their parent's choice of DVD, before giving in and agreeing to watch the chosen movie. Mr Jones' often used threat of either watching the film or going to bed tended to settle any arguments.

On the way home the family would then stop to pick up a takeaway to eat while they watched the film. The choice of takeaway, however, was also the cause of many a Friday night squabble between the siblings. Alfie preferred pizza, while Megan liked Chinese. Sometimes Mr and Mrs Jones wondered why they bothered.

However, on this particular Friday night, Megan was staying at a friend's house while Mr and Mrs Jones were going out, so for once Alfie was allowed to choose his own DVD and takeaway.

To neither of his parent's great surprise, Alfie chose to order a cheese and tomato pizza from his favourite takeaway outlet and, rather than picking a film to watch, he chose instead to hire out a DVD which, according to the display box, showed '200 of the best football goals from around the world'.

Alfie wanted to put the DVD on the very second he got home from the shop, but he was told by his parents that he first had to spend some time with his Nan, who would be looking after him that evening. Normally Alfie wouldn't have minded spending time with his Nan, but he was still on a high from scoring five goals in the tournament earlier that day and all he wanted to do was watch, and think, about football.

It didn't take Alfie's Nan long to see that his heart wasn't really in playing with her that evening so, almost as soon as Mr and Mrs Jones left the house, she let him put the DVD on.

" Thanks, Nan. You're the best," said Alfie, giving her a great big hug.

"That's okay, dear. I'll be in the kitchen tidying up if you need me. I honestly don't know how you all manage to make so much mess in there, really I don't!"

Alfie smiled to himself. His Nan was always moaning about how messy their house was and she tended to spend most of her visits tidying up one room or the other. His Mum and Dad pretended to get angry about her "interfering ways", but he knew they were secretly glad that she did it. After all, it saved them a job.

The DVD was even better than Alfie had hoped it would be. He watched so much football, either on the television or on his Dad's computer, that he was certain he would have seen most of the goals somewhere before, but so far he'd sat through 89 goals and hadn't previously seen any of them.

Goal number 90, however, was a fairly recent effort scored by one of Alfie's favourite England players. He had seen this goal many, many times before but had no problem watching it again. It was the best goal that he had ever seen in his life – a perfectly executed overhead kick from the edge of the penalty area.

Alfie watched in anticipation as England's right midfielder got the ball by the corner flag. He knew exactly what was about to happen. The winger would nutmeg his marker before sending over a deep cross that would only be half cleared by an opposition defender. In the blink of an eye the England centre forward, who was standing with his back to goal, would then throw himself backwards, almost performing a reverse somersault, and the ball would leave his boot as if it had been shot out of a cannon, giving the stunned goalkeeper absolutely no chance of saving it.

Sure enough, the winger put the ball through the legs of his opponent and crossed the ball, just as Alfie had known he would. The defender did then indeed manage to get his head ever so slightly to the ball, only managing to deflect it towards the England striker who then flung himself acrobatically at it.

But this time the striker didn't score. In fact, he didn't even manage to get his foot on the ball. He simply missed it completely. The ball landed harmlessly at the feet of a relieved defender who managed to clear it.

Alfie was stunned. He rubbed his eyes in disbelief. He couldn't believe what he was seeing. He'd seen that goal dozens of times. He knew that the striker scored. Why else would it be on a DVD showing 200 of the best goals from around the world?

He reached for the remote control. Goal number 90 was at the start of one of the DVD's chapters so he could watch it again without much of a problem. He was just about to press the back arrow button when the screen suddenly went blank.

'I don't believe it,' Alfie thought to himself. 'The disc is broken. It's not fair'. He was just about to call his Nan to tell her that something had gone wrong with the TV, when the picture reappeared just as quickly as it had vanished.

However, to Alfie's utter amazement, it was no longer images of footballers scoring goals that occupied the television screen.

It was the face of someone that Alfie hadn't seen for more than eight months.

Chapter three

Alfie couldn't prise his eyes away from the television screen. For one whole minute he just sat motionless on the sofa, helpless to do anything but stare at the familiar face that was looking back at him. He tried changing the channel on the TV but the picture on the screen wouldn't alter, no matter which button he pressed.

Finally the silence in the room was broken by a voice coming from the TV. "Hello, Alfie. Long time no see."

The voice belonged to Madam Zola, a mysterious old fortune teller whom Alfie had befriended the previous December at a fun-fair. In their first meeting the old lady had amazed Alfie by knowing simply everything there was to know about him. She had then really caught the young boy's attention by telling him that it was his destiny to become a professional footballer, providing he stayed playing for the Kingsway Colts – something that hadn't appeared very likely at the time.

Over the weeks that followed, Alfie had seen the fortune teller on a number of occasions and he was convinced that it was only with her help that he was able to get the better of his arch rival, Jasper Johnson, and stay a Colts player. Not that he knew how, or even why, she had helped him.

The last time he had seen Madam Zola was on Christmas Eve, and although he was always fairly sure that he would see her again one day, he never in a million years would have guessed that she would turn up on the television screen in his parent's front room.

Yet here she was looking right at him. And not only was she looking at him, she was talking to him, too.

Alfie rubbed his eyes again. He felt like he must have been dreaming, but he knew he wasn't. This was really

happening. Madam Zola was back.

After a short period of even more silence, the fortune teller began to laugh heartily. "Oh I wish I could see your face, Alfie," she said. "I bet it's a real picture. Unfortunately I can't see you from in here, but I can hear you. So are you pleased to see me Alfie?"

Forgetting for a moment what Madam Zola had just told him, Alfie merely nodded his response. It wasn't until the fortune teller began looking at her wrist as if to check on the time – even though she wasn't wearing watch – that Alfie remembered what she had said.

"Err... yes," he finally replied, just about managing to force the words out. He was still in something of a state of shock.

"Well it's good to see you, too, Alfie. Not that I can see you, of course, but you know what I mean." The fortune teller looked at her watchless wrist again. "Oh my, is that the time already. Doesn't time fly when you're having fun? Anyway, enough of all this small talk. Are you looking forward to this Sunday's football tournament in Ashgate?"

By now Alfie was slowly starting to get over the shock of seeing Madam Zola again. He wasn't in the least bit surprised that she knew he was due to be playing in a football competition that Sunday. She knew everything about him.

"Yeah, I can't wait," said Alfie, starting to relax.

"Even though it will mean playing against Jasper again?"

Although Alfie hadn't known for sure that Jasper would be playing in the tournament, he was not at all surprised to hear that his former teammate would be there.

The two boys both attended the Kingsway Junior School, and Jasper had spent the last few days of term before the summer holidays boasting about how his new team would "easily thrash the rubbish Kingsway Colts," and that this would happen "really, really soon."

Jasper had left the Colts just before Christmas, after Alfie had beaten him in a one-on-one game of football. Since then, Jasper and his Dad – the Colt's former coach, Keith – had spent almost eight months forming a new team made up of as many of the best soon to be under 10s players in Kingsway and its surrounding areas as they could find. Unsurprisingly, they hadn't asked any of the Colts players to join them. They knew the answer would be 'no'.

Alfie shrugged his shoulders at the television screen and then instantly remembered that Madam Zola couldn't actually see him. "It doesn't bother me at all," he said confidently. He meant it, too. Since Alfie had defeated Jasper in their one-on-one match, his confidence had soared, and he was no longer scared of Jasper – despite the fact that his former teammate was far bigger than he was.

"I'm glad to hear it," the fortune teller replied with a big smile on her face. "But playing against Jasper again will be the least of your worries at the tournament."

"What do you mean?" Alfie asked, although he didn't really expect the fortune teller to answer him – Madam Zola liked to keep him guessing.

Therefore he wasn't surprised by Madam Zola's response. "I don't really have the time to explain right now," she answered hurriedly, once again glancing down at her bare wrist. "Let's just say that it's vitally important that you never judge a book by its cover. Failure to realise this could have dire consequences for you and your destiny."

The fortune teller looked down at her wrist again. "And with that I really must be going. I've been here for far too long already."

"But, Madam Zola, what do you mean don't judge a book by its..." Alfie started to ask. But it was too late. Before he could finish his sentence the television screen had gone blank again and the fortune teller had disappeared.

For around 30 seconds, Alfie sat motionless. He continued staring at the blank television screen, thinking about what Madam Zola had just said and trying to work out what she might have meant. However, no matter how hard he tried to work it out, he simply didn't have a clue what the fortune teller had been talking about – and he had even less of an idea of what he was supposed to do about it.

So lost in thought was Alfie, that he hadn't even noticed that the DVD had started working again. It was only when the crowd on the TV roared with delight as a stunning overhead kick beat the goalkeeper that Alfie remembered what he had been watching less than five minutes ago.

He had just missed his favourite goal.

Chapter four

After the excitement of seeing Madam Zola again, Alfie hardly slept a wink that night. By the morning he still didn't have a clue what the fortune teller might have meant by not judging a book by its cover. As if that wasn't bad enough, he was now really tired, too.

So tired, in fact, that he twice nearly fell asleep at the breakfast table.

"Are you alright, darling?" a concerned Mrs Jones asked her son the second time she noticed his eyes starting to droop.

"Yeah, fine. Just a bit tired," Alfie answered while stretching and yawning.

"Are you going to be well enough to go to football training this morning? You don't seem quite right to me."

"Hmmm, yep," Alfie replied, even

though he hadn't really heard what his Mum had just asked him. He'd been too busy trying to keep his eyes open to be able to actually concentrate on what Mrs Jones was saying.

By the time his parents had dropped him off at Billy's house, Alfie was starting to feel a bit more awake, although he still had huge bags under his eyes and he hadn't bothered to comb his blond mop of curly hair, meaning it looked messier than usual.

"Morning, Alf. You don't look too good," said Billy upon seeing his friend.

"I'm alright. Just a bit tired. I didn't sleep very well last night," Alfie replied whilst trying, and failing, to stop himself from yawning yet again.

"Is it because of the tournament tomorrow? Are you feeling a bit nervous?"

"Yeah, a little bit," Alfie lied. Although it wasn't nerves that had kept him awake, he had decided to tell Billy it was as Madam Zola had once warned him not to tell anyone else about her. He also knew how stupid it would sound to other people if he told them that he knew a magic fortune teller who had told him it was his destiny to be a professional footballer. Even Billy probably wouldn't believe that.

"I just hope we beat Jasper's new team," Alfie added, waking up a little at the thought of the following day's tournament.

"If Jasper's new team are even going to be there," replied Billy. "Chloe told me that they only had six players before the summer holidays started. She said that Jasper was boasting about how they were waiting for a really amazing player before picking a seventh."

"Oh, he'll be there," Alfie stated, knowingly. "I'm certain of it."

"How can you be so sure? Jasper hasn't spoken to you once since you beat him in that game."

"I just know, okay."

Billy was just about to push his friend further on why he was so certain Jasper would be at the tournament, when Mr Morris knocked on the door of Billy's bedroom to tell the two boys that he was ready to take them to training.

Mr Morris nearly always took Alfie and Billy to training and matches as Alfie's parents didn't really like football and tended to take Megan to her activities instead. She was currently taking horse riding lessons having got bored of doing ballet after only a few months.

There was a really excited buzz amongst the Colts' players as they arrived at the Kingsway Recreation Ground that particular Saturday morning. None of the children had ever played in a real tournament before, and they were all really looking forward to the next day's event. Because of the high excitement levels, however, there was more messing around than usual and Jimmy had to stop the training session on three separate occasions to try and get the children to concentrate. This was something he very rarely had to do.

It was only when he split the squad into two teams for their end of training match that the Kingsway players decided to stop messing about and started to take the session seriously. Jimmy hadn't really minded all the mucking about, though. He had coached youth football teams for many years and had seen this kind of excitement plenty of times before. He totally understood it. He was looking forward to the tournament himself.

At the end of training, Jimmy announced that all eight players in the Colts' squad would be involved in the tournament, meaning that the team would have a sub for each game. The elderly coach then explained that there would be six group games and that he would change the team around in every game so that nobody was sub more than once. He also asked for volunteers to be goalkeepers; but as he had fully expected, only Pranav Jamal raised his hand.

Although Jimmy firmly believed in giving all young players the chance to play in different positions, he had always struggled to get children to go in goal – especially in this particular team. However, as Pranav loved being in goal and none of the other players did – especially Alfie who absolutely hated it – he'd given up trying to rotate his goalkeeper and had said that Pranav could be the goalkeeper for every match providing that no one else wanted to have a go. They never did.

Just as Jimmy was finishing off his end of session talk, the children became distracted by the sound of a car pulling speedily into the car park and then screeching to a halt.

Without even having to look round, all eight Kingsway players instantly knew exactly who had just turned up. Keith and Jasper Johnson. This was the way they had always turned up to training and matches when they had been part of the Colts. Just so everyone knew they were there.

Sure enough, within seconds, both of the car's front doors flew open and out stepped the all too familiar father and son duo.

"What do they want?" Chloe moaned.

"Maybe they've come to ask Billy to play for their new team," suggested Liam, only half joking.

"No way," said Billy. "I'd never play for them. I've already told Jasper that at school."

"Don't worry everybody. I'm sure we're just about to find out what they're doing here," said Jimmy calmly, as he watched the pair approach.

"Morning losers," bellowed Keith cheerfully, a wide smile spreading across his round, red face.

Nobody responded. They just stared back at Keith and his son.

"What, you're not even going to say hello?" Keith continued. "That's not very nice is it, son? Here we are just stopping by to say hello to some old friends and they're ignoring us. That's a bit rude if you ask me."

"It's very rude, Dad," agreed Jasper.

From the moment they had approached the Colts players, Jasper had not once taken his eyes off Alfie, and even as he spoke he continued glowering at his nemesis.

Alfie tried to avoid making eye contact with the larger boy, looking everywhere he possibly could to evade Jasper's scowl. Although he was not really that scared of him anymore, Alfie couldn't help but feel a little intimidated by Jasper's presence. It seemed to Alfie that his rival had actually gotten bigger since the end of the school term. Something he hadn't thought was possible.

"What do you want, Keith?" Jimmy snapped, not even trying to hide his dislike of the former coach from the children.

"I don't want anything," Keith replied in a friendly tone of voice, the wide smile still fixed firmly on his face. "Me and Jasper just wanted to come and wish you good luck for tomorrow's tournament in Ashgate... after all, if you come up against our team you're going to need all the luck you can get."

"That's very kind of you," Jimmy replied, clearly not meaning a word of what he said.

"What's up, old man? You don't seem very pleased to see me."

"Just go away, Keith. If we play you tomorrow, we'll see who the best team is then."

"Oh, don't worry old man. We already know who the best team is... and it certainly isn't you. Come on Jasper, let's go."

Jasper had continued to stare at Alfie throughout the whole exchange between Jimmy and Keith. It was only moments before Jasper turned to follow his Dad back to the car that his facial expression changed for the first time.

Alfie had looked up just in time to see a sinister smile appear on his rival's face. A smile that Alfie had seen many times before. One that meant Jasper had a plan in mind.

Alfie felt his heart start to thud hard against his chest and his legs started to shake ever so slightly. Now he really was beginning to feel nervous about the following day's tournament.

Chapter five

Alfie didn't particularly like reading books. He didn't mind reading football magazines but books just took too much time, effort and concentration to bother with. And there weren't enough pictures, either.

Alfie would do anything he possibly could to avoid sitting still for too long. He had once volunteered to help his Mum tidy the house just so that he wouldn't have to read a chapter of a book for his homework.

So you can probably imagine Mr and Mrs Jones' surprise when they went into Alfie's room that Saturday evening and saw him frantically picking up and looking at the books that sat on his largely unused bookshelves.

"Erm, what are you doing, Alf?" a clearly confused Mr Jones asked his son.

"Nothing, Dad," answered Alfie without averting his eyes from the books.

"Are you looking for something in particular, darling?" enquired Mrs Jones, sounding just as confused as her husband.

"Not really," replied Alfie as he took yet another book off the shelf, looked at it and then placed it on the floor in a pile with the others that he had already glanced at.

"Are you looking for a book to read?" Mrs Jones continued. "Because I think there's one in your school bag that you're supposed to be reading over the summer holi..."

"No, don't be silly. Of course I'm not looking for a book to read, Mum. I'm not mad or anything... or bored. Well, not bored enough to read a book, anyway."

"Then just what are you doing?" both parents asked at exactly the same time.

For the first time since Mr and Mrs Jones had entered his room, Alfie stopped taking books from the shelves and turned to look at his parents. "What does it mean when someone says that you shouldn't judge a book by its cover?"

"Well, Alf, it means that even though a book's cover may not look that interesting, the story may actually turn out to be really good and exciting."

Alfie stopped to think about this for a moment. He had been hoping that by looking at the covers of all his books he might have been given a clue as to what Madam Zola had been talking about the previous night. Realising that Jasper had a plan in mind for the next day's tournament, Alfie believed that he simply had to work out what she meant as quickly as possible.

"But all books are boring," he said after

a while, still none the wiser as to what the fortune teller's mysterious message was supposed to mean. "Some look exciting from the cover, but then you open them and... it's just words. Boring."

Mr Jones smiled. "Not all books are boring, Alf. But yes, it can work the other way, too. So a book that may look good might turn out to be bad or..."

"And it's just an old saying," chirped in Mrs Jones before Mr Jones could finish his sentence. This was something she did quite often. "It could mean books, it could mean films, or food, or shops, people... almost anything, in fact"

"Do you mean I've been looking at all these books for no reason?" Alfie asked, sounding horrified that he may have just wasted half an hour looking at books. Well, the covers of books.

"Well, we don't really know, darling," answered Mrs Jones. "We're not really sure what you're doing. What are you doing?"

"I heard Chloe's Mum say to Billy's Dad that you shouldn't judge a book by its cover, and I was trying to work out what it meant," Alfie fibbed. "And now you're telling me that she might not have even been talking about books! She really is a strange old woman," he added, as he thought about Madam Zola and of how he still wasn't any closer to finding out what she had been talking about.

"Alfie! That's no way to talk about Mrs Reed," snapped Mr Jones angrily.

For a moment Alfie didn't know why his Dad had got so angry, but he quickly realised that Mr Jones still thought he'd been talking about Chloe's Mum. "Err, sorry. I didn't mean that," he apologised as his cheeks started to redden. "Please don't tell Chloe's Mum I called her strange. Or old!"

Both Mr and Mrs Jones laughed. "We won't," continued, Mr Jones. "But I don't want to hear you being that rude about her again. Or anyone else for that matter."

"I won't. Sorry Dad."

"That's okay. Anyway, we just came up here to tell you that it's nearly bedtime. So put your pyjamas on, go and clean your teeth and then you can watch TV for a little while. You don't want to be too late to bed tonight. You've got that big tournament thingy tomorrow."

"But I still need to work out what Madam Z... I mean Mrs Reed meant," explained Alfie. He knew he was fast running out of time to solve the fortune teller's latest riddle.

"We've already told you what she meant. Now go and clean your teeth."

After another minute or two of trying to persuade his parents to let him stay up a little bit later, Alfie gave up arguing and slowly made his way down the hall to the bathroom.

It was while he was brushing his teeth that something Mrs Jones had said a few moments earlier came back to him. The phrase 'you shouldn't judge a book by its cover' didn't only have to apply to a book. It could mean other things, too... including people.

And suddenly Alfie was certain that what Madam Zola had told him didn't have anything to do with books at all. She had been warning him to not judge another person too quickly. But who was she talking about? And why?

Alfie had a feeling it wouldn't be too long before he found out.

Chapter six

For once, Alfie and Billy were not the first
to arrive at the ground the following day.
Usually, Mr Morris always got the two
boys to wherever they were playing extra
early as he was constantly worried that
there would otherwise be lots of traffic
and they would end up being late.

Although Mr Morris had, as ever,
arrived to pick Alfie up ten minutes
earlier than he had said he would, on
that particular morning he and Billy were
kept waiting for Alfie, who was frantically
searching his room for his lucky mascot.

Alfie's lucky mascot was a small teddy
bear which wore a blue football kit, just
like the one worn by the Kingsway Colts.
It had been given to him by Madam Zola
during one of their first meetings and the

young boy had put it in his boot bag for every game he had played ever since.

He was convinced that it was a magic bear, although he had never told anyone about it. Not because Madam Zola had warned him not too, but because he was worried his teammates would laugh at him for carrying a teddy bear around with him.

Eventually, after turning his bedroom upside down looking for it, and having accused Megan of taking and hiding it, Mrs Jones had found it exactly where he'd left it – in his old boot bag; the one he hadn't used since the Colts' last proper match back in early April.

Because of the search for the bear, Mr Morris's car hadn't left the Jones' household until the time when he was actually supposed to pick Alfie up, and so Jimmy Grimshaw, Des Grey, Pranav and Liam were already at the ground by the time Mr Morris's car pulled into the Ashgate Community Park's car park.

"Wow this must be a first," laughed Jimmy as Alfie and Billy wandered over to join their coach and friends. "I don't think I've ever arrived at a ground before you two."

"Sorry, that was my fault," said Alfie. "I

couldn't find my shin pads."

Jimmy laughed again. "That's alright, Alfie. You're still here in plenty of time. We'll just wait for the other three to arrive and then we'll have to go and sign in over there," the old coach said, pointing towards a huge blue tent. "We'll also find out what teams are in our group then."

"I hope we'll be playing Jasper's new team," said Pranav. "I'd love to beat them. Him and Keith would be really gutted if we did."

"Yeah, me too," agreed Billy. "Do you know what his team is called?"

"Probably the rejects," joked Liam, prompting Pranav, Des and Billy to all laugh out loud. Even Jimmy had a slight smile on his face.

Alfie, however, kept quiet. He didn't laugh or smile at the joke. Ever since he had come to the conclusion that Madam Zola had been warning him not to judge people too quickly, he'd spent a lot of time thinking about who she could have actually been talking about.

And the more he thought about it, the more he convinced himself that she must have been talking about Jasper. The truth was that Jasper hadn't actually been nasty to him once since before Christmas. Okay, so he hadn't actually spoken to him in all that time, but still... Maybe his former teammate had changed for the better.

Could Alfie have imagined the evil smile on Jasper's face at training the previous day? He didn't think that he had, but he couldn't be 100 per cent sure. He'd been tired, after all. He was almost certain that Madam Zola's warning must have applied to Jasper.

Within minutes, the five Colts players and Jimmy were joined by the three remaining team members – Chloe, Danny Foreman and Luke Stanford. Luke was the newest Kingsway player and probably the weakest footballer in the squad. However, he tried his hardest in every game, no matter what position he was playing in and he was well liked by all of his teammates.

"Come on then everyone, let's go and tell the organisers that we're here and find out what pitch we're playing on," said Jimmy. "Hopefully on one of the closer ones. I don't think my legs could take it if we were on one of the far pitches, especially not in this heat," he added.

Ashgate Community Park was one of

the biggest parks in the entire area that surrounded Kingsway and there were a total of 24 mini-soccer pitches dotted throughout the grounds. It was a blazing hot day and as they walked to the blue organisers tent, Jimmy had to keep reminding his team how important it was that they kept drinking plenty of water and made sure they rested in between games.

The closer they got to the tent, the more excited the children became about finding out who they would be playing and what time their first game would be. Just then, Alfie spotted Keith and Jasper, both of whom had already seen the Colts arrive and were now heading towards the group.

"Morning losers," Keith said cheerfully. "You'll be pleased to know that you won't be facing the mighty North Malling Town today as we're not in your group."

There was a collective sigh of disappointment from all of the Colts players, apart from Alfie, at the news that they wouldn't be playing Keith and Jasper's team.

Again, Jasper hardly spoke. He just stood staring at Alfie with a serious look on his face. Alfie was almost convinced that the larger boy was trying to intimidate him, but he was trying his hardest to give Jasper the benefit of any doubt. 'Maybe he's just concentrating really hard,' Alfie thought to himself, although he was struggling to believe that this was really the case.

"Of course, we could always end up playing each other in the semi-final or final," continued Keith. "But let's face it... you're not going to get that far, are you?"

"Let's just see what happens, Keith, shall we," replied Jimmy, as coolly as he possibly could. He was determined not to let the younger coach get under his skin today in the way that he had at training a day earlier.

"I guess we shall," Keith agreed. "Come on Jasper. Let's leave these losers to it. We need to go and get prepared. See you later losers."

With that, Keith and Jasper walked off towards where a group of five other boys wearing the same red and black striped kit as Jasper were sat. They were all massive for their age, far bigger than all of the Colts' players aside from Danny. Danny was one of the tallest boys in his school, although he was as skinny as a rake.

"That's strange," stated Chloe as she

watched Jasper join his new teammates.

"What's strange, Chloe?" Jimmy asked.

"Well, there are only six players on the North Malling team. That means they'll be a player short and won't have any substitutes."

"Keith hardly ever uses his substitutes anyway," remarked Alfie bitterly, as he recalled all the times his former coach had made him sub and then not brought him on.

"They're still a player short, though," said Chloe.

"Maybe they never found that really good seventh player that Jasper kept going on to you about," offered Billy by way of explanation.

Before Chloe had a chance to answer, Jimmy raised his right hand as a signal to silence his team. While the Colts players had been chatting between themselves, Jimmy had popped into the blue tent to sign his team in and had come back with a fixture list. "Let's not worry about how many players Keith's team may or may not have," he said. "Let's concentrate on our own game and make sure we enjoy our first taste of tournament football."

All the Colts players nodded and then,

seeing that their coach was holding the fixture list in his right hand, demanded to know who they were playing first.

"We've got a team called Rickton Rovers in 30 minutes," answered Jimmy. "Thankfully we're only on Pitch Three which is that pitch there," he continued, pointing to the pitch next to where Keith and Jasper's team were gathered. "There's a game on before us, so we'll all sit down and watch that and then I'll tell you what the team for the first match will be."

The Colts players all cheered and rushed off to find a spot in the shade as close to the pitch they would be playing on as they could.

As they ran towards the pitch, Alfie accidentally bumped into another boy and knocked him over.

"Sorry, I wasn't looking where I was going," said Alfie, offering the other boy his hand to help him up. The other boy just ignored him, though, and stood up by himself before turning away from Alfie without so much as uttering a single word.

It was only then that Alfie recognised who he had bumped into.

"You're not going to believe this," said

Alfie, rushing over to sit next to Billy. "That miserable Hayden boy from the course is here!"

"Oh no," said Billy shaking his head. "I hope he's not playing for a team in our group. He's well good. Where is he?"

Alfie craned his neck to search for the sullen boy and quickly spotted him. "Over there," he said pointing to where the boy was standing.

Billy looked around just in time to see Hayden remove the black tracksuit top he had been wearing.

Billy and Alfie both looked horrified as they noticed Hayden's red and black striped football shirt.

North Malling Town's seventh player had arrived.

Chapter seven

Jimmy read out the team for the first game and Alfie was delighted to hear that he would be starting the match in left midfield. Pranav was in goal, Danny and Luke in defence, Billy right midfield, Chloe in the centre and Liam striker. Des was sub, but he didn't mind as he knew that meant he would be starting the next game.

"The games are only six minutes each way, so they are much shorter than what we're used to," explained Jimmy in his pre-match team talk. "That means that there probably won't be too many goals scored in any of the games here today, so if we're going to win then scoring first will be important. We've never played Rickton Rovers before so we don't really know what they are going to be like, but let's not worry about that. Let's do what we do best – work hard and try to play good football. Give it your best shot and try to win. But if we do lose then don't worry. Just so long as you go out there and enjoy it."

None of the Colts players said anything. They just nodded at their coach. Now that the first game was fast approaching they were all starting to feel a little bit nervous – even more so than usual. They had never played in a match for league points before as all of their previous games had only been classed as 'friendlies'. Although they just wanted to go out onto the pitch and enjoy the match like they normally did, they couldn't help but feel a little bit more anxious about this game than they ever had before.

Soon enough the referee's whistle sounded to end the first game that had been being played on Pitch Three, meaning that it was time for the Colts' opening match.

The Kingsway players had been disappointed to learn that North Malling's first game was on at the same time as theirs so they wouldn't be able to watch their former coach's new team in action. But now that it was actually match time, none of the Kingsway players were even thinking about Jasper and Keith. They were all fully concentrating on their own game.

Once the game started it was immediately obvious that the Colts were feeling tense. Straight from the kick off Liam passed the ball back to the normally reliable Danny who, instead of controlling and passing it as he would usually have done, put his foot straight through the ball in an attempt to clear it up-field. He succeeded only in slicing the ball off the pitch for a Rickton throw-in.

Then, from the throw in, Chloe tried to win the ball from the player she was marking, but only ended up needlessly fouling her opponent. Less than 30 seconds had been played and already Rickton had a free-kick in a very dangerous position.

After a brief disagreement between two Rovers players about who should take the free kick, the opposition's number four picked the ball up and carefully placed it where the foul had been committed.

He then took five steps back before running up and pelting the ball as hard as he could. The ball flew past Alfie and

Luke who had formed a wall to try and block the shot, and it was only a fantastic save from Pranav, who just about managed to get his fingertips to the ball, that stopped Rickton from taking a very early lead.

But they did have a corner.

Again it was the number four who took it, but this time he did not strike the ball so cleanly and it rolled harmlessly to Billy's feet. However, even the Colts' star player was feeling nervous, and rather than clear the ball or dribble it upfield, he tried to do something he'd been told countless times before that he should never attempt. He passed the ball straight across the face of his own goal.

Although he'd been trying to pass to Alfie, who was standing in plenty of space on the left touchline, Billy hadn't been at all aware of the other players around him. The pass was easily intercepted by the Rickton number eight who couldn't believe his luck. Pranav, who hadn't expected Billy to pass the ball across his own goal, was caught badly out of position, and the number eight had plenty of time to slot the ball into the empty goal. The Colts were losing and barely a minute had been played.

Unsurprisingly, conceding an early goal did little to boost the team's confidence. For the next four minutes it was only a combination of bad finishing from Rickton's striker and two more good saves from Pranav that kept the Colts in the game.

Kingsway only managed to create one chance in the opening six minutes, and that came in the very final minute of the half. By this point the Colts were finally starting to overcome their early nerves and for the first time they actually managed to put together a good passing move which ended with Liam shooting inches wide from just inside the penalty area.

The effort seemed to give the Colts players the added belief that they so desperately required. Straight from the goal kick, Alfie won the ball back, but before he had time to do anything with it the referee blew his whistle to signal half-time.

"Wow, that half went so quickly," said Billy as the Kingsway players got into a huddle around Jimmy and started drinking some much needed water.

"I told you that the time would go fast," said Jimmy smiling. Although the Colts weren't playing at all well Jimmy wasn't angry with them. He very rarely got angry just so long as they all tried their hardest. Which they all were. "I don't need to tell you that you can all play better than that," he continued, his voice remaining calm. "It's obvious to see that you were all a little nervous at the start but the one time you managed to get the ball down and play football you nearly scored. So let's forget about that half now. Go out and there and enjoy the next six minutes and we'll see what happens."

The second half could not have been more different from the first. Whether it was Jimmy's words of encouragement or merely the fact that the Colts had now almost completely forgotten about their initial nerves, there was no doubt that Kingsway looked a far better side after the break.

Liam and Billy had already gone close to equalising when Luke won a 50/50 tackle on the halfway line. The ball rolled through to Chloe who played a brilliant first time pass to Billy. The right midfielder jinked his way past two opponents before sending over a perfect cross towards Liam. The Colt's goal machine stretched for the ball knowing that even the faintest touch would be enough to send the ball past the Rickton 'keeper. Unfortunately for Liam his leg just wasn't quite long enough for him to be able to get a toe on the ball. Fortunately for the Colts, though, and especially for Alfie, it rolled straight to the back post where he was waiting to prod the ball over the line. 1-1

All of the Colts' players, including Pranav, mobbed Alfie and the watching Colts' parents shouted their approval from the sidelines.

With three minutes left there was still enough time remaining for either team to win the match.

However, although the games were much shorter than what the players on both sides were used to, the weather was also much hotter to what they were used to playing in as well, and ultimately neither team had the energy to chase a winner.

At the end of the game both teams were happy with a draw. As Jimmy had said to his players before the match, in such a short format not many goals would be scored so a draw was seen as an okay result – especially as two sides from each seven-team group would go through to the semi-final. They still had five games to get the results they needed.

Jimmy congratulated all of his players on their efforts and urged them to all sit down and drink some water. But before any of the Colts' could even think about sitting down they first wanted to find out how Jasper's new team had got on.

The eight children all rushed over to see what was happening on the other under 9s pitch. The game there had also just finished but all of the Kingsway players could tell that North Malling had won just from seeing the smug look on Keith's face.

"What was the score?" Alfie asked one of the other team's players, who looked absolutely shattered.

"We lost 5-1," he replied, gasping for breath. "Their number 9 is amazing. He scored all five!"

The Colts' players didn't need to look to see who was wearing the number 9 shirt.

With Hayden Whitlock on their team North Malling Town were going to be very, very hard to beat indeed!

Chapter eight

Kingsway's next two games also ended in draws, with both matches finishing without any goals being scored.

The Colts were playing well enough by now, but were finding it quite hard to create goal scoring chances in the short games.

At the halfway point of the tournament's group stage, the Colts were in fourth place with three points from three games, although two of the teams ahead of them in the table – Ashgate Athletic and Rickton Rovers – had played one fewer game than Kingsway.

"We need to start scoring some goals soon otherwise we'll never make it to the semi final," said Billy to Alfie as the two boys looked at the latest league table, which was pinned to a board next to the organisers' tent.

To make matters worse, Keith and Jasper's North Malling Town team were having no such problems in front of goal. Largely thanks to the individual brilliance of Hayden. So far they had won all three of their games, scoring nine goals in the process. Hayden had scored eight of those goals with Jasper scoring the other from the penalty spot. He had insisted on taking the penalty, even though Hayden had already scored two in the match and only needed one more for yet another hat-trick.

The Colts' next game was against Lakeland Spurs who were bottom of the group having lost two matches and drawn one. Kingsway had played Lakeland twice before during the previous season and had beaten them both times, so they were confident they could win this match.

However, Jimmy then surprised everyone in the Kingsway squad when he read out the team for the Lakeland game. Billy was sub.

"But we have to win this match if we're going to go through," moaned Alfie. "We need Billy to play otherwise we might only draw again – or maybe even lose."

"Why?"" Jimmy asked, quizzically. "I've told you time and time again that you're all as good as each other and that you should have more confidence in your own ability. I told you yesterday that everyone, apart from Pranav, would take a turn at being sub and it is now Billy's turn. It's only fair."

Billy didn't say anything and although Alfie opened his mouth to plead with Jimmy not to make his best friend sub, at the last moment he decided against doing so. He was worried the coach might make him sub instead.

'At least we've still got Liam as striker,' Alfie thought to himself as he made his way onto the pitch for the start of the game.

Although it was supposed to have been Liam's turn to be in defence, Luke had asked Jimmy if he could play at the back again as he thought it was his best position. Jimmy had tried to insist that Luke at least tried to play up front, but Luke eventually persuaded the coach to let him swap places with Liam. It kept both boys happy and, in the end, that was good enough for Jimmy.

Alfie was also playing in defence for that game and, although it wasn't his favourite position, he didn't mind playing there too much. He may have been one of the smaller boys in his year at school, but he liked getting stuck in. What's more, ever since he'd beaten Jasper in their one on one match he hadn't been so intimidated about coming up against bigger opponents.

As it turned out, though, Alfie spent most of the match going forward. Lakeland were not a particularly good side and Kingsway were almost continually on the attack. With Luke happy to stay back and defend, this allowed Alfie to move into midfield and help Des out in the centre of the pitch.

Even without Billy's sublime skills, Kingsway were still able to create plenty of chances and any worries they may have had about their star player not playing were eased when Chloe and Liam played a quick one-two on the edge of Lakeland's penalty area in a move which led to the Colt's only female player slotting the ball past the Spurs goalie. 1-0 to the Colts.

By half-time Pranav still hadn't touched the ball, but despite the fact the Colts were in complete control of the game Jimmy warned his players not to gct complacent. "They may only need one chance to score, so it's important we try and get a second goal," he warned. "If they score first then the whole game could change."

With Jimmy's warning still ringing in their ears, the Colts' players laid siege to the Spurs goal in the second half. Danny and Des both missed good chances to score before Chloe was denied a second goal by a brilliant save from the Lakeland goalkeeper.

With time running out it seemed that Chloe's first-half strike would be enough to keep Kingsway in with a chance of qualifying for the semi-finals. With just over a minute remaining, Kingsway had a corner kick. Alfie knew that a goal here would surely win the game for the Colts so, despite Luke telling him to stay back and defend, he decided to go forward to try and score his second goal of the tournament.

It was a bad decision. A very bad decision, indeed.

Des's corner kick was superbly held by the Lakeland goalkeeper, who was easily his side's best player. Straight away he sent a big kick up field to where Luke was now outnumbered two players to one.

Realising his mistake, Alfie rushed back as fast as he could to help out his teammate.

He was too late.

One of the Lakeland players had got to the ball first and as Luke went to tackle him the Spurs' player produced a good pass to send the other attacker clean through on goal.

Pranav came out of his goal to try and narrow the attacker's shooting angle, but the Lakeland player still managed to send a great shot screaming past one of Pranav's outstretched arms.

Alfie covered his eyes with his hands. He couldn't bear to see ball hit the net. He knew that it was his fault Luke had been left with two players to mark and felt terrible that his error had cost the Colts' their place in the tournament.

But instead of hearing the cheers of the Lakeland players and parents celebrating a goal, Alfie instead heard a loud thud. He quickly removed his hands from his eyes. The ball hadn't hit the net at all. It had crashed off the post and was now at the feet of Luke who had fortunately not given up his pursuit of the Spurs' forward.

Knowing there wasn't long left Luke

hoofed the ball forward, not wanting to invite any further pressure on his team's goal. Although he hadn't meant it, his clearance actually turned into a fantastic pass, bypassing all of Lakeland's defence and finding Liam who had stayed forward from the corner. If there was one player the Colts could have possibly wanted to be clear through on goal in the last minute of a game it would be Liam.

He didn't let his teammates down.

Determined not to give Lakeland's goalkeeper the chance to demonstrate his impressive shot saving ability, Kingsway's top scorer instead decided to take the ball round the onrushing goalie before stroking it into the unguarded goal.

At 2-0, with less than 30 seconds left, the Colts' victory was secured.

In spite of Alfie's error, Kingsway were still in with a chance of qualifying for the next round.

Chapter nine

As soon as the final whistle sounded all
eight of the Kingsway squad rushed over
to the board near the organiser's tent to
see how their victory had affected the
league table.

It took the organisers a few minutes to
update the table. They has to wait for
the referees from each game to confirm
the scores from their matches before they
could make the necessary changes.

Once the scores were finally in the news
was not particularly great for the Colts.

Rickton Rovers had beaten Heath Hill
United 1-0 to leave them with seven
points from three games, while Ashgate
Athletic had defeated Southfield United
3-0 to make it three wins out of three for
the tournament's host team.

However, Southfield had been third in the league before the fourth round of matches so, although the Colts may not have closed the gap on the top two teams, they had at least moved into third place.

"We're only one point off of second," said Liam, as he studied the updated league standings. "We can still qualify."

"Yes, but Ashgate and Rickton have still only played three games and we've played four," Chloe pointed out. "So even if we beat Ashgate we still need to hope that one of the other teams can beat them or Rickton as well."

"When are we playing Ashgate?" Billy asked his teammates.

"It's our next game," said Liam, who always seemed to know who was playing who and when.

"Wow," said Billy, puffing out his cheeks. "That's going to be a really hard game. I remember when we played Ashgate last season. We beat them 3-2 in one game and they beat us 4-1 in the other."

Alfie couldn't help but smile at the thought of playing against Ashgate.

His Mum and Dad had almost made him join them the previous season when Keith had been treating him so badly. He wondered how it would have felt to have been playing against his friends in this important match rather than with them. If it hadn't have been for Madam Zola it could well have happened.

The Colts' players were just about to go back to the area where Jimmy and their parents had set up a couple of small tents to help shield the children from the scorching sun, when Keith and Jasper, along with some of the other North Malling Town players, wandered over to look at the league tables.

While Kingsway had been beating Lakeland Spurs 2-0, North Malling Town had kept their impressive start to the tournament going by beating Brook Wanderers by the same score. Hayden had once again been North Malling's hero, having scored both the goals. The win meant that Keith and Jasper's team were the first under 9s side to qualify for the semi finals.

"Oh dear," said Keith as he spotted the children he had once coached. "Oh dear, oh dear, oh dear. Not looking too good for the Clots... I mean the Colts... Is it Jasper?"

"No it isn't Dad," replied Jasper, who had already started staring menacingly in Alfie's direction.

"Looks like we won't be meeting you lot in this tournament after all," continued Keith. "Just like I said we wouldn't. I knew you lot wouldn't qualify. Not with Old Man Grimshaw and his silly ideas about playing football for enjoyment. You see, boys and girls, sport is all about winning. You'll learn that one day. The biggest mistake you lot ever made was choosing Jimmy over me."

"We're not out yet," snapped Chloe, irritably. "We're only a point behind second place."

"You'll never beat Ashgate," said Keith, shaking his head, a smug smile plastered across his face. "You only managed to beat them last year because Jasper was playing. I heard that you got thrashed once we had left. You've got no chance of getting through."

Although it was true that Jasper had played in the Colts' narrow win over Ashgate, the reason they had lost the return game so heavily undoubtedly had more to do with the fact that both Liam and Chloe had missed the match due to a stomach bug, as opposed to Jasper's absence.

But before any of the players had a chance to argue this point, Keith and his son had already started to move off in the direction of the stalls selling refreshments.

As they marched past their former team, Jasper made a point of deliberately bumping his shoulder into Alfie with just enough force to send the smaller boy spinning, but not quite enough to knock him over.

"I don't really care about winning this tournament," said Billy, once the father and son were out of earshot. "But I'd sure love to beat them. You alright, Alf. That was out of order what Jasper just did."

"Yeah, he's a real idiot," added Danny.

The other Colts players nodded in agreement.

So they were somewhat shocked by Alfie's response.

"Nah, Jasper's alright. I'm sure he didn't mean it. I think it was an accident."

From the moment Alfie had got away with his mistake in the previous game, he had become further convinced that he'd been right about Madam Zola's warning. She had been advising him not to judge Jasper. That for some reason his former teammate was misunderstood and didn't really mean to be quite as nasty as he seemed – as hard as that was to believe.

He was sure that keeping an open mind about Jasper would not only help the Colts win the tournament, but would also somehow aid him in fulfilling his destiny of one day being a professional footballer. He trusted Madam Zola and would do almost whatever she told him, providing it kept his dream alive.

"Okay, Alf, if you say so," said Billy, who couldn't quite believe his best friend was sticking up for Jasper. "But it would be great to beat them, wouldn't it?"

Alfie shrugged his shoulders. "I guess," he replied. "But we've got to get past Ashgate to even stand a chance of qualifying for the semis. And like you said, that's going to be tough."

"Come on then," said Billy to all of his teammates. "Let's get back to the tents. It can't be that long till the next... wait a minute, where's Des gone?"

"He's over there," said Pranav, pointing towards one of the refreshment stalls. "Talking to one of the North Malling players."

"Des come on," shouted Liam at the top of his voice. "We need to go back and get ready for the next game."

Des quickly finished his conversation

with the other boy and ran over to rejoin his friends.

"What are you talking to that lot for?" Liam asked Des as the team walked back to their makeshift base. It was obvious that Liam was not too pleased to see his teammate talking to one of Keith's players.

"Because he's my friend," answered Des innocently. "He goes to the same Cubs group as me on a Monday. He's alright. He's nothing like Jasper."

"If you say so," snorted Liam, who couldn't quite believe that anybody who played for North Malling could be 'alright'.

Des ignored the angry tone in Liam's voice. "He was just saying that they're only doing as well as they are because of that Hayden. He says he's really good at football, but that he doesn't speak to anyone and doesn't celebrate when he scores. Even when he gets a hat-trick."

"He was like that on Friday at the course we were at, wasn't he?" said Chloe to Liam, Billy and Alfie.

The three boys nodded. "He does seem a bit odd," agreed Billy.

The Colts' players looked over to where the North Malling team had been sitting in between games. Sure enough, there was Hayden, sitting all alone around ten yards away from where the rest of his team's bags and belongings were positioned.

However, it wasn't the fact that he was sitting all by himself which seemed odd to Alfie. It was more the fact that Hayden seemed to be staring right at him.

There was something about the look on Hayden's face that Alfie didn't like. Or trust!

Chapter ten

"We all know it's going to be a hard game," said Jimmy as he came towards the end of his pre-match team talk. "But all I ask from each of you is that you go out there, try your best and most importantly..."

"ENJOY IT," the Kingsway players all shouted together. Nearly all of Jimmy's team talks ended with these two words. The elderly coach smiled broadly as his players finished the talk for him.

Despite the importance of the game against Ashgate, the Colts seemed far more relaxed than they had been before the opening game of the tournament. Jimmy was fully confident that his team could give themselves a chance of qualifying for the semi-finals with one game still to play – although he knew that whether they would actually get through the group or not would still depend on other results.

For the time being, Alfie had managed to push his concerns about the way Hayden had been looking at him to the back of his mind. He was really looking forward to the game.

He was in a particularly buoyant mood as it was his turn to be up front. He loved playing as a striker. As this meant it would be his turn to be sub for the last group game, Alfie was determined to do everything that he possibly could to give his teammates a chance of reaching the semi finals.

The referee was just about to get the game underway when the Kingsway players heard a familiar voice shouting from the sidelines. "Alfie's playing in attack? Oh dear, oh dear. You've got no chance of reaching the semi finals, then!" It was Keith.

For the first time that day, the Kingsway Colts and North Malling Town games were not kicking off at the same time, so Keith, Jasper and a few of the other North Malling players had moved over to Pitch Three to watch the Colts in action. Hayden was not one of the other players watching, though, Alfie noted with interest.

He also realised that Jasper, alongside one or two of the other boys, were laughing at what Keith had shouted. In spite of this, Alfie was still determined not to jump to any conclusions about Jasper. 'Keith is his Dad,' he said to himself silently. 'He's got no choice but to laugh, I suppose.'

As soon as Jimmy had seen Keith appear on the opposite sideline to where he was standing, Kingsway's coach had sensed that there could be trouble. He immediately went and spoke to the watching parents of the Colts players, asking them not to get involved with Keith. Jimmy reasoned that this was exactly what the former coach wanted as it would act as a distraction to the Kingsway players.

Begrudgingly, the parents agreed not to say anything, although Mr Morris was particularly unhappy about having to keep silent while Keith deliberately tried to put off his son's team.

The game kicked off and, despite Keith's taunting, the Colts started the match well.

Having been sub in the previous game, Billy was well rested and from his position in the centre of midfield he was causing Ashgate's defence plenty of problems. He almost scored twice in the first three minutes. Once with a long-range shot that went just wide, and again when he dribbled past three players only to then shoot straight at the opposition's grateful goalkeeper.

Alfie was also playing well. He didn't let Ashgate's defenders have a moment's peace, continually closing them down whenever they had the ball. He was also linking up well with the Colt's midfield trio of Chloe, Billy and Des whenever Kingsway were attacking. In defence, Danny and Luke were proving to be a solid partnership and Pranav had yet to touch the ball.

However, despite the Colts' dominance, aside from Billy's two early chances they didn't really look that much like scoring. As half-time approached Keith and his watching team were continuing to ridicule the Kingsway players at every opportunity.

Billy's shot wide had been met with a chorus of jeers by the watching North Malling Town players who had then started singing 'how wide do you want the goal', while every time Alfie touched the ball Keith made a negative comment just loud enough for the young boy to hear.

The watching Colts parents were becoming increasingly frustrated with Keith and his team's antics, and it took all of Jimmy's calming presence to stop them from confronting the North Malling Town coach.

As soon as the half-time whistle sounded the Kingsway players rushed over to Jimmy who, for the first time that day, had positioned himself a fair distance away from the parents. He didn't want their anger rubbing off on his team. A calm head was definitely needed in this situation.

"This is so unfair," moaned Chloe as she approached her coach.

"Yeah, Keith's putting us off on purpose," whined Danny. "It's well out of order. We'd be winning this game if it wasn't for him and the rest of his team."

Jimmy smiled warmly at his players. He could see that all of them were upset by what was going on off the pitch, even Liam who was substitute. But he knew that it was vital for him to keep their confidence levels up and he needed to try to get them to stop thinking about Keith and Jasper. "Yet you're still all playing really, really well," he said, trying to offer encouragement to his dejected team. "Ashgate are a really good team, yet you've hardly given them a kick of the ball. Pranav hasn't even had a touch yet. That's how on top you are."

"But we're not winning. We need to win otherwise we're out," replied Chloe, miserably.

"And if we play like that again in the second half we will win," Jimmy reassured them. "We need to try to have a few more shots on goal. Our passing and movement is brilliant but, as I told you earlier, the game times are so short that the first goal is vital. Let's try to be a bit more direct this half and try and test their goalkeeper."

"But if we miss then the North Malling boys will all laugh at us," said Billy, remembering the chanting that had been aimed at him after he'd shot wide in the first half.

"And if you score what will they say then?" Jimmy asked.

"Nothing, I guess," answered Billy, shrugging his shoulders.

"Exactly," responded Jimmy enthusiastically. "If we score, then there will be nothing they can say. Just keep ignoring the taunts, like you have been, and continue playing good football. That's the best way to get Keith and Jasper to keep their mouths shut."

"It's not really Jasper," chirped up Alfie, taking all of his teammates by surprise. "I mean, he's not that bad, is he? I haven't really heard him say anything nasty."

There was shocked silence as his friends and coach just stared at him. They couldn't quite believe what they were hearing.

Eventually, it was Billy who broke the uncomfortable silence. "Did you not hear him taking the mickey out of me when I shot wide? Why do you keep sticking up for him, Alf? Especially after how horrible he's been to you in the past."

It was a question Alfie couldn't really answer.

The more he saw Jasper that day, the more difficult it became for him to not judge the former Colts' captain as still being the bully he knew so well, but Madam Zola's words were still ringing in his ears – 'don't judge a book by its cover.'

Alfie decided it was best not to say

anything at all and instead just gave a half-hearted shrug of his shoulders by way of response.

"Let's try and forget about Keith and Jasper Johnson for the next six minutes," continued Jimmy, desperately trying to get his team's focus back on the game. "Remember what I've just said. Be more direct and try to test their goalkeeper. Now let's get going. We've got a game to win."

Chapter eleven

Never in a million years could Jimmy
have imagined that his half-time words
would have been quite so well received by
his players.

Straight from the restart, Alfie passed
the ball to Billy who, just as he had at the
beginning of the first half, decided to take
on the Ashgate team by himself.

He used a combination of skill and
speed to get past two players and take
the ball to the edge of the penalty area.

Two more Ashgate players ran towards
the Colts' number seven in an attempt
to close him down. But Billy had already
moved the ball onto his preferred right
foot and, before his opponents could get
within five yards of him, he had sent a
shot arrowing towards the top left-hand

corner of the goal. He could not have dreamt of hitting a better shot and he was already heading off to celebrate with the rest of the Colts players when, somehow, the Ashgate goalkeeper, stretching as if he was made of elastic, managed to tip the ball over the bar.

Even the watching North Malling Town players and coach had to admit that it was a brilliant strike and that the Colts had only been denied a goal by an amazing save. Not that any of them would ever dream of saying so out loud, of course.

From the resulting corner, Chloe hit the ball hard and low, aiming for Alfie at the front post. Although he was beaten to the ball by his marker, who just managed to get his toe to it before Alfie could get there, the clearance only went as far as Des who was standing just outside the area.

Without even taking a touch to control the ball, Des swung his right boot and connected with it perfectly. The goalkeeper didn't even see the ball coming towards him but to his great relief, and the Colts' disbelief, he heard the ball canon off the crossbar and then saw it bounce away to safety.

The Kingsway players couldn't quite believe that the game was still goalless. All eight of the Colts' squad had their hands on their heads and were cursing their bad luck.

Jimmy, however, was obviously delighted with what he was seeing. His team had listened to exactly what he'd asked of them at half-time, and within a minute of the restart they had twice gone close to opening the scoring.

Not only that, but Keith, Jasper and the other North Malling Town players had, for the time being at least, stopped jeering his team.

"Keep your heads up, Kingsway," cheered Jimmy, clapping his hands together enthusiastically. "You're playing really well. Keep it up."

Within seconds the Colts once again got hold of the ball in a promising position. Chloe played the ball short to Alfie who then played a great reverse pass to Billy. For the umpteenth time in the match Kingsway's star player set off towards the opposition goal, leaving Ashgate players trailing in his wake. He burst into the area before squaring the ball across the goal to Des who shot first time, just as he had a few moments before.

Once again the Ashgate goalkeeper was left helpless by the strike, but the Colts players could only watch in dismay as the ball thundered against the outside of the right-hand post and went out for a goal kick.

For the next minute or so not much happened as both teams began to tire. Keith once again started to find his voice, making spiteful comments every time a Colts player made even the slightest error. Jimmy could see the confidence begin to drain out of his players. No one wanted to have a shot or take an opponent on for fear of missing the target or being tackled.

Unsurprisingly, Kingsway began to get sloppy and started to panic, hoofing the ball upfield instead of playing the good quality football that they were well capable of. Even Billy was giving the ball away almost every time he got it. Something he very rarely did.

"How long left?" Alfie asked the ref as an Ashgate player raced to get the ball which Danny had just hopelessly sliced off for a throw-in when under no pressure whatsoever – much to Keith, Jasper and co's obvious delight.

"Just over two minutes," said the ref.

Alfie shook his head. He could see no way that his team were going to get the win they so desperately needed. Since the three quick chances they'd created at the beginning of the half the Colts hadn't even gone close to scoring. As Keith's taunts had grown louder and louder, the teams performance had got worse and worse.

As Alfie waited for the Ashgate defender to retrieve the ball he took a quick glance in the direction of Keith and Jasper. It didn't surprise him to see that both father and son were grinning from ear to ear, evidently enjoying the fact that their old team were only minutes away from being eliminated from the tournament.

What did surprise Alfie, though, is that the watching North Malling Town players had now been joined by someone else. Although he sat a little way apart from the rest of the group, Hayden was also now sitting by the side of the pitch. Unlike his coach and teammates, he was not laughing and joking around. In fact, he didn't even look like he was paying that much attention to anything that was going on around him. As far as Alfie could tell he was just sat there, staring at the ground.

As Alfie continued to stare in his direction, Hayden looked up and for the briefest moment the two boys shared direct eye contact before the North Malling player quickly looked away to resume gazing at the grass.

There was something about Hayden that Alfie didn't like. He always looked so sullen and miserable and on the few occasions that Alfie or one of his friends had made an effort to talk to him he'd just been plain rude. The fact that Hayden was playing for Keith's new team hadn't endeared the newcomer to Alfie, either. Nor had the fact that he was so obviously brilliant at football.

'He just thinks he's so much better than everyone else,' Alfie angrily thought to himself as the Ashgate defender finally made his way back to the pitch with the ball.

Alfie could suddenly feel adrenaline pumping throughout his whole body. Whereas only moments before he had found jogging to be hard work, he now felt fully revitalised and ready to run again.

It was almost as if he'd been powered up like a toy that's just had its batteries replaced. He was determined to show

Hayden just what he could do with a football at his feet.

Having had to run so far to get the ball, the worn out Ashgate defender's throw-in was weak and Alfie managed to intercept the ball before it reached its intended target. Without pausing for thought he brought the ball under control and began to sprint forward with it, finding a turn of pace that even he didn't know he possessed.

The opposition players had been used to Billy running at them, but hadn't expected Alfie to do the same. He was usually content to tackle and pass, so his sudden surge forward had caught the defenders flat footed.

He burst past the halfway line, keeping the ball under control superbly. Those watching the run could have been forgiven for thinking that the ball was attached to one his bootlaces.

The Ashgate players tried desperately to catch and tackle him, but Alfie just sprinted past all of them, swerving this way and that to bamboozle anyone who stood in his way. Within seconds of winning the ball, Alfie had made his way from deep inside his own half to the edge of the opposition's penalty area and he was now through one-on-one with the Ashgate goalkeeper.

The 'keeper came out of his goal in an attempt to narrow the shooting angle, but Alfie had expected him to do so and had already decided on his next move.

For the first time since starting the run Alfie let the ball get away from his feet. Believing that he had miscontrolled the ball at the vital moment, the goalkeeper went down to gather it, but quick as a flash, Alfie used his other foot to move the ball to the side of the now grounded 'keeper.

The goalie grasped at nothing more than air and Alfie casually sidestepped past him to be left with the simple task of tapping the ball into the unguarded net.

There was a moment of stunned silence before the Colts players and their watching parents went absolutely crazy. Alfie was mobbed by all of his teammates, including substitute Liam, while the parents cheered louder than any of the team could remember them having done so before. Even Jimmy was jumping up and down like a hyperactive yo-yo, clearly caught up in the moment.

Through the crowd of players that were bundled on top of him, Alfie spotted

Jasper and Keith. They weren't smiling anymore. They simply looked stunned. He quickly peeked at where Hayden had been sitting, but all he could see there now was an empty space.

'Please tell me he saw that,' Alfie thought to himself as his teammates finally clambered off him so that they could finish the game. Despite the elation he felt at having scored such a wonderful – and important – goal, there was a small part of Alfie that would have been gutted if Hayden hadn't actually seen him score it.

The final minute or so of the game rushed by without any further chances for either team. And when the referee's whistle blew to bring the match to a close, Kingsway had done what they needed to do. They had won the game.

With just one match remaining the Colts' were still in with a chance of qualifying for the semi-finals.

Chapter twelve

"It's going to be really close," said Billy as he examined the latest league table.

He wasn't kidding. There were now only three teams in the group left with a realistic chance of qualifying; Rickton Rovers, Ashgate Athletic and Kingsway Colts. Only one point separated them.

	P	W	D	L	F	A	Pts
Rickton Rovers	4	3	1	0	4	1	10
Ashgate Athletic	4	3	0	1	8	2	9
Kingsway Colts	**5**	**2**	**3**	**0**	**4**	**1**	**9**

"Rickton and Ashgate both have a game in hand, though," moaned Liam, who was fearing that, in spite of the team's best efforts, Kingsway would still fall short in their bid to qualify for the semi-finals.

"Yes, but they have to play each other in

the next game when we play Southfield United," said Chloe confidently. "So if they draw and we win, then we'll be top of the group!"

"Yes, but they'll still have one game left and we would have played all of ours," continued Liam, his tone of voice becoming ever gloomier. "Either team would still only need to win their last game to qualify no matter what the score is when they play each other."

"Hmmm... well, at least we've still got a chance," replied Chloe, although she too was now sounding far less confident than she had been just seconds earlier.

Alfie hadn't once taken his eyes off the league table from the moment it had been updated. He was trying to work out all the possible results that would give the Colts the best chance of qualifying. But as Liam had already pointed out, no matter what happened in the next round of games, the Colts' fate would still rely on Rickton and Ashgate's other result.

"Hey, Alf, you coming to watch North Malling's game on Pitch Four?" Billy asked his friend as the Kingsway players began to move away from the organiser's area.

"Yeah, I'll be over in a minute, I just

want to check one more thing."

"It doesn't matter what you check, Alf," laughed Billy. "We need to win and then hope another team can do us a favour."

"I know," Alfie frowned. "But I still want to check."

Billy chuckled. "Okay, Alf, but don't be too long. Even though Jimmy's warned us not to say anything out of order while watching North Malling, he didn't say anything about not pulling funny faces to put them off. Not that you get a much funnier face than Keith or Jasper's anyway."

Alfie couldn't stop himself from smiling, even though he knew he shouldn't. "Cool, I'll be over in a minute."

As Billy ran off in the direction of Pitch Four, Alfie took one more look at the league table. His friends were right. There was nothing Kingsway could do to ensure they qualified. They just had to try their hardest to win their last match and then hope for the best.

Having finally given up on finding a hidden way through to the semi finals that no one else had spotted, Alfie decided to go and join his teammates watch the North Malling game.

"I bet Hayden can't score a goal as

good as I just did," Alfie said to himself, proudly.

As he turned to make his way towards Pitch Four, however, Alfie accidentally banged his leg against a table, sending a box of pens scattering everywhere.

"Sorry," he quickly called out before one of the stern looking tournament organisers had a chance to moan at him. "I'll pick them up."

Fortunately, most of the pens hadn't gone far and it didn't take him too long to find them all. "There you go," said Alfie placing the pot of pens back on the table.

"There's still one missing," complained one of the organisers without even glancing up from the newspaper he was reading. "I think the other one rolled into the tent."

Alfie sighed loudly. He was sure that he'd picked up all of the pens, but rather than argue he decided it would be quicker to just go and have a look inside the tent.

He pulled back the canvas door and walked in. As he suspected there was no pen on the floor. Just a table with lots of boring looking tournament entry forms on it.

He turned to leave the tent but was stopped in his tracks by a familiar sound.

He stood perfectly still, wanting to hear it again. He wanted to be certain that he'd heard what he thought he had.

However, after half-a-minute of standing as still as a statue he could hear nothing other than the noise of children playing football coming from outside the tent. Nothing unusual at all.

He went to leave again, but at the very moment he placed his hand on the tent door he heard the same sound he thought he'd heard moments earlier. And this time it was getting louder.

There was no mistaking it now. It was a sound he remembered only too well.

Wind chimes.

It was a noise that could mean only one thing.

Madam Zola was nearby.

Chapter thirteen

While he was standing motionless by
the tent's door, Alfie cast his mind back
to the first time that he'd ever met the
mysterious fortune teller.

On that occasion the sound of wind
chimes starting up had terrified him.

He had been standing in what he had
believed to be an empty tent at a local
fun-fair when, all at once, loads of wind
chimes, which had been hanging from the
ceiling, had begun to clang. The din they
had made had been deafening.

Seconds later smoke had flooded the
tent and when it cleared Madam Zola had
been standing right in front of him.

The sound of wind chimes had also
heralded her arrival when he'd met her
at a Santa's Grotto and in a shop at the

Kingsway Shopping Centre. So when he heard the wind chimes this time he was fully prepared to see her again.

He turned around to face the table which had all the team's entry forms placed in piles on it. To his surprise, the fortune teller was nowhere to be seen.

Alfie scratched his head. He felt, and indeed looked, extremely puzzled. He had been sure that Madam Zola was going to be standing behind him. He walked up to the table to see if anything looked different up close.

It didn't.

The sound of wind chimes continued to echo throughout the tent even though Alfie could not see any hanging anywhere.

"Hello," Alfie called out at the top of his voice. "Madam Zola, are you here?"

There was no answer.

Feeling confused and frustrated, Alfie once again turned to leave the tent, but as he did so the noise being made by the invisible wind chimes became even louder.

The noise was so loud that Alfie jumped backwards in shock and for the second time in the space of a few minutes he bumped into a table.

Two pieces of paper fell from the table and fluttered slowly to the floor. Alfie bent down to pick them up and just as he did so the wind chimes stopped clanging, much to his relief.

The young boy was just about to put the pieces of paper back on the table when he noticed something strange. His name was written on the top piece of paper. Nothing else. Just his name.

Alfie's blue eyes opened wide in astonishment. He could not believe what he was seeing. Alfie slowly turned the piece of paper over. There was nothing at all written on the other side.

He looked at the second piece of paper that had fallen on the floor. Once again there was only one name written on it.

"Hayden Whitlock," Alfie said aloud, as he read the name that was written on the piece of paper. "What is going on?"

Alfie started rummaging frantically through the other forms on the table. They were all normal entry forms which had been filled in by every team that was taking part in that day's tournament.

"What do you think you're looking at?" yelled a voice from behind Alfie.

He spun around instantly, fearing he was just about to be told off by one of the tournament organisers for being somewhere he shouldn't be. He was about to explain that he was still looking for the missing pen, when he saw who it was that had spoken.

"Hello, Alfie. How are you?"

Although just moments earlier Alfie had been fully prepared to meet Madam Zola once again, given what had just occurred he was now shaken and it took him a good few seconds to regain his composure.

He was sure the voice that had just shouted at him had belonged to a man, but there was no question of who was now standing in front him.

"M... M... Madam Zola," he just about managed to stutter. "What's going on? Why are you here? Why is my name written on one piece of paper and Hayden Whitlock's on another? And just where are those wind chimes that were making so much noise?"

Madam Zola smiled warmly at him. Her kind brown eyes twinkled. "My dear boy, so many questions, so little time for answers."

Alfie glared at Madam Zola. Although he was by now used to her obscure ways, at that particular moment he was not in the mood for games.

"Oh don't frown, Alfie. It really doesn't suit you," the fortune teller continued. "Now, how are you? I hear you scored a great goal in your last game. Well done. You must be very proud. So what is it you are doing here?"

Alfie was stunned. Not by the fact that she knew he'd just scored a great goal – she was bound to know that, she knew everything about him – but that she was asking him what he was doing there.

"What do you mean what am I doing here? I'm playing in a football tournament, you know I am," he replied, trying his hardest to stay calm.

"You're playing in a football tournament inside this tent?" Madam Zola asked, sounding genuinely confused.

"What? No! Of course not in this tent. Out there," Alfie answered, pointing in the direction of the tent's door.

"So why are you in here when all your teammates are out there?"

"I knocked a pot of pens over and came in here to pick one up. Then I heard wind chimes and I realised you must be around here somewhere."

"Wind chimes?" Madam Zola repeated, again sounding confused. "I didn't hear any wind chimes. Well I never, that is strange isn't it?"

Alfie shook his head. He was really starting to run out of patience with the fortune teller. "Look, Madam Zola, I don't mean to be rude but do you have something you'd like to tell me? If not I'd really like to go back and watch Jasper's game with my friends."

The old lady suddenly looked very sad. "That's the problem with the youth of today. You're always in such a rush. No time to speak to the elderly. Oh well." Madam Zola let out a big sad sigh and then smiled at Alfie again. "Anyway I just came to say hello. I saw you run into this tent so thought I'd follow you in here rather than embarrass you in front of all your friends. I thought you liked seeing me."

Alfie felt bad. He hadn't meant to hurt her feelings. The truth was he really did like seeing the fortune teller, even if she did drive him crazy sometimes with her cryptic messages.

At the same time, he was also a little confused. Usually it was Madam Zola who was always in a rush to get somewhere, not him.

"I'm sorry," said Alfie, "I just thought you might have had another message for me."

"No, Alfie. Not today. Anyway, you had better run along now otherwise you'll miss the rest of the game. I'm sure I'll see you again soon."

Alfie hesitated. He felt really guilty that he'd been so rude to the fortune teller, especially as she'd done so much to help him out in the past. "I am really sorry, Madam Zola, I didn't mean to..."

"That's fine, Alfie," the fortune teller said reassuringly. "It was nice to see you again."

"Yeah, it was nice to see you, too."

Alfie wanted to go and give Madam Zola

a big hug, but he felt a little awkward about doing so. It's not like he knew her that well. In the end he decided just to wave and walk past her.

He was just about to leave the tent when Madam Zola spoke again.

"Hayden Whitlock?"

Alfie turned around to face the fortune teller. "Pardon?" he asked.

"Did you say something a little earlier about Hayden Whitlock?"

"Yeah. His name is written on a piece of paper over on the table. And so is mine. Why?"

"Have you met him? Isn't he a nice young boy? So polite and well mannered. He's a bit like you, really."

Alfie was perplexed. She couldn't possibly be talking about the same boy. "That's not quite what I'd say. I don't really like him that much to be honest."

For a brief moment a flash of anger worked its way across Madam Zola's face. She then looked quizzically at Alfie. "Why ever not?"

"Dunno really. He just seems really rude and miserable all the time."

"Do you know him well?"

Alfie shrugged his shoulders. "Not really. I only met him for the first time on Friday, but he's so unfriendly. And if that's not bad enough he's playing for Jasper's team today. And he's really good at football."

Madam Zola glowered at Alfie. "Well I am very disappointed in you. Do you not listen to anything I ever tell you? Oh dear, oh dear. Such a shame. It would be horrible if you didn't fulfil your destiny because of this. Oh dear, oh dear."

The fortune teller looked at her wrist. As ever, there was no watch on it but that didn't seem to matter to Madam Zola. "Is that the time already! Well, I can't be hanging around here all day. Chatter, chatter, chatter that's all you ever do, Alfie. I'm late now. I really must be off."

Madam Zola marched past Alfie to the tent's door. The young boy was too confused to say anything. He couldn't think straight. "You really need to listen to what I say, Alfie," said the fortune teller once again, and then she was gone through the door and out of sight.

Alfie was just about to turn and chase after her when, suddenly, he realised his mistake. The fortune teller hadn't been warning him not to judge Jasper at all.

She'd been warning him not to judge Hayden.

Chapter fourteen

By the time Alfie finally rejoined his
friends by the side of Pitch Four, the
North Malling Town game was nearing
full-time.

"Where have you been, Alf?" Billy asked
as he saw his best friend approach.

"Erm, just..."

"You haven't been studying the league
table all this time, have you?" Liam
chuckled.

"No, I was just... Erm..."

Billy could see that there was something
not quite right with his buddy. "Are you
okay, Alf? You look like you've seen a
ghost."

Alfie smiled but said nothing.
Sometimes he wished he could tell Billy
all about his meetings with Madam Zola.

But he knew that he couldn't. He'd been
warned not to and that was one thing
he was definitely going to listen to the
fortune teller about.

"Yeah, I'm fine. Just a bit nervous about
our next game," Alfie fibbed. "It's a really
important one for us."

Liam laughed again. "It's your turn
to be sub, Alfie. You don't need to be
nervous."

"I know, but still..."

Alfie settled down on the floor next to
Billy. He looked up just as Hayden had
the ball at his feet. The Kingsway players
watched in awe as the North Malling

player took on and beat three players before shooting just wide.

"Ohhh, that was close," said a clearly impressed Chloe. "That would have been his hat-trick. They're winning 2-0 by the way, Alfie."

Alfie nodded his acknowledgement. Hayden was an amazing football player, there was no doubt about that.

Even Keith was being careful not to upset Hayden in the same way he used to aggravate the Kingsway players. "Unlucky Hayden. Just keep on giving him the ball lads," the coach shouted.

"He would have had a go at one of us for missing that," moaned Billy. "He would have said that we should have passed to Jasper."

All the Kingsway players agreed with Billy. The memories of how unfair Keith was to each of them – especially Alfie – when he was the Colts' coach were still fairly fresh in all of their minds.

"I'm so glad you beat Jasper in that one-on-one match, Alfie," said Pranav. "My Mum and Dad were going to make me leave if Keith stayed as our coach."

"Mine too," said Billy and Danny together.

"Hmmm. Cool," replied Alfie who wasn't

really paying much attention to what was being said. His thoughts were elsewhere.

Ever since Madam Zola had walked out of the tent he had been going over things in his mind. It now seemed so obvious to him that the fortune teller had not been talking about Jasper when she had warned him not to judge a book by its cover.

He'd known Jasper long enough to realise what an unpleasant boy he was. The way his former teammate had been acting towards him over the past couple of days should have been all the proof he needed that Jasper hadn't changed.

He'd also been trying to imagine what it must be like to be Hayden. Alfie and his friends had been told that Hayden had only recently moved to Kingsway from Norton. The new boy hadn't known anyone else at the football course they had been on, and he was obviously quite a shy boy.

Alfie thought about what it would be like if he moved to a new town where he didn't know anybody. He wouldn't like that at all.

Alfie was so lost in thought that he didn't even realise the final whistle of the North Malling game had sounded. It was only when Billy tapped him on the shoulder that he became aware that most of his teammates had already rushed over to Pitch Three where their match was due to begin shortly.

"Come on, Alf," said Billy offering out his hand to help pull his friend up. "Don't look so concerned about the next game. We'll be fine."

"Yeah, I know," Alfie replied as, with Billy's aid, he got to his feet. "I'm just thinking about how great it would be to get through and beat Keith and Jasper's team in the semi-final or final."

Billy nodded. "That would be amazing," he agreed. "But with that Hayden in their team I don't really see how we can beat them."

Alfie looked across to where the North Malling players were gathered. Most of them were celebrating yet another win – their fifth out five in the tournament so far. But once again Hayden was all alone, not even looking in the direction of his teammates and coach. He still looked miserable.

"He's a bit odd, isn't he?" said Billy as he noticed the direction in which Alfie was looking.

"I'm not sure," Alfie replied. "I've got a

feeling that he might actually be alright. Maybe we should try talking to him again."

"If you say so. But it will have to wait until after our next game. Look, Jimmy's waiting for us over there so that we can get started. Come on I'll race you."

Without giving his friend the chance to respond, Billy sped off in the direction of Jimmy and the rest of the Colts. Alfie took one more look at Hayden, then set off in pursuit of his best friend.

He didn't know what he would actually say to Hayden when the time came, yet he couldn't help but feel that his next conversation with the newcomer would be a very important one.

Chapter fifteen

The Colts couldn't have wished for
a better start to their match against
Southfield United.

They had taken the lead in less than a
minute following a calamitous mistake
from the opposition goalkeeper. A long
range shot from Billy had been heading
way off target when, rather than letting
the ball roll harmlessly wide for a goal-
kick, the 'keeper instead decided to
dive on the ball and gather it into his
body. However, he'd made a real hash of
bringing the ball into his chest and only
managed to knock it back into the danger
area where a waiting Liam had gratefully
accepted the gift and fired the Colts into a
1-0 lead.

Since that early goal, though, Southfield

had spent much of the match piling pressure on the Kingsway defence and it was only thanks to some goalkeeping heroics from Pranav that the Colts had maintained their one-goal advantage.

Alfie had spent much of the game with his hands covering his eyes, watching what was going on through tiny gaps inbetween his fingers. Although he didn't mind taking turns at being sub, he simply hated the feeling of helplessness he was getting from watching his friends battle to stay 1-0 up and being unable to do anything about it himself, except shout encouragement.

'Come on ref,' he muttered nervously to himself as yet another Southfield shot was well dealt with by Pranav. 'It must be nearly half-time now. Just get to half-time 1-0 up and then Jimmy will tell us what we need to do to make sure we get the win we need.'

Alfie peeked over at Jimmy. As ever, the elderly coach was smiling and full of encouragement for all of his players. Alfie couldn't help but wonder how his coach always managed to stay so calm. None of the other team's coaches ever looked so relaxed. They were always prowling up and down the touchline, screaming instructions and orders to their players; celebrating wildly when their team scored and generally looking disgusted when they let a goal in.

Jimmy very rarely moved from the same spot throughout the game and his facial expression seemed to be locked on a permanent smile no matter what was happening.

The elderly coach noticed Alfie looking at him. "It's a bit tense, isn't it," he chuckled. "Still, it's all good fun."

Jimmy turned back to watch the game. Alfie shook his head and smiled. Although he sometimes found it hard to agree with Jimmy's opinion that having fun was far more important than winning, he realised that Jimmy truly did believe this to be the case. The coach didn't really mind how the team got on, just so long as his players were enjoying themselves.

After what seemed to Alfie like the longest half of football that day, the whistle finally blew for half-time. The Colts had just about managed to cling onto their early lead.

Jimmy's half-time team talk was short. He praised his players for the effort they were all putting in and then urged them to try and keep possession of the ball a little bit more. "We're panicking too much at times," he said. "You're all good enough players to get the ball under control, get your head up and pass it to a teammate. Do that for the next six minutes and keep the effort of the first half going, and we'll win this game."

The players all nodded and were just about to retake to the pitch when Liam asked Alfie if he knew what the score of the game between Rickton Rovers and Ashgate Athletic was.

Alfie had been concentrating so hard on his own team's first half that he'd completely forgotten that the top two teams in the group were currently playing against each other. However, sensing that he might be less nervous watching that match rather than his own team's he offered to go and find out.

The Rickton against Ashgate game was being played on Pitch One, which was located about 20 yards immediately behind Pitch Three. Jimmy considered Alfie's offer for a moment. "Hmmm, I suppose there would be no harm in you going over there quickly to find out what's going on. But don't be too long and keep an eye on me just in case I need to bring you on."

Alfie agreed and quickly headed off in the direction of Pitch One. He was pretty sure that, unless there was an injury to one of his teammates, he wouldn't be needed by Jimmy. The games were so short that the coach had stated before the very first game of the day that he wouldn't make changes unless someone was hurt or too tired to continue.

The Ashgate vs Rickton game must have kicked off a few minutes earlier than Kingsway's as when Alfie got to the pitch the game was already midway through the second half. "What's the score?" he asked one of the watching parents.

"0-0. It's a really good game, though," came the reply.

Alfie had spent enough time studying the latest league table to know that this was exactly the result the Colts wanted. If the scores of both matches stayed the same then that would put Kingsway top and mean that, providing either one of Ashgate or Rickton failed to win their final game, his team would be through.

Alfie glanced back at Pitch Three. His teammates had only just started their second half and Jimmy did not seem too concerned by his sub's whereabouts.

'I'll just stay and watch the end of this

game,' he decided to himself.

The parent he had spoken to had been right. Despite the lack of goals this was a really good game. One moment Ashgate were on the attack and seconds later Rickton were.

Alfie saw the referee look at his watch – something he knew they did when it was nearly full-time. 'Time to head back,' he thought to himself. 'What a great result this is for our chances of qualifying.' Although he'd been really enjoying the match he was watching, he had kept enough of an eye on what was going on in his own team's game to know that the Colts were still winning.

He began jogging back to Pitch Three when, much to his dismay, he heard a huge shout come from the direction of Pitch One. "PENALTY!"

Alfie turned around instantly, only to have his worst fears confirmed. He had been sure that the game must have been all but over but the referee had awarded Rickton a very, very late penalty.

The Ashgate players were not at all happy about the decision and in the end their coach and some of the parents had to step in to move their players away from the ref. Alfie stood halfway between the two pitches, wishing with all his might that Rickton would miss.

He was not to be so lucky.

The same player that had scored against the Colts earlier in the day stepped up and confidently slammed the ball past the Ashgate goalie to surely win the game for his team.

Indeed, by the time the Rickton players had finished their celebrations, Ashgate barely had time to kick off before the ref finally blew his whistle to bring the match to a close.

Alfie once again began to walk back to his own pitch. He was desperately trying to work out what that result would now mean for his own team when, to his disbelief, he looked up just in time to see Luke give the ball away right on the edge of his own penalty area.

Once again, Alfie covered his eyes with his hands and peeked out. Unlike in the first half, though, this time Pranav couldn't save his side.

The Southfield striker finally managed to beat the Colts' shot stopper to score a deserved equaliser for his team.

Alfie put his hands on his head as all of his teammates slumped to their knees. Luke was almost in tears and it took all of Jimmy's encouragement to gee his team up so that they could restart the game.

Alfie began to run towards Jimmy, keen to try and lift his teammates for one final push. However, he had barely reached his coach before the referee blew for full-time.

Two last gasp goals in two separate matches had left Kingsway's hopes of qualifying for the semi-final hanging by the thinnest of threads.

Chapter sixteen

Only Liam had gone over to the organiser's area with Jimmy to view the newest league table. None of the other Colt's players could quite bring themselves to look at it – they all feared that Southfield's last minute goal had totally blown their chances of qualifying for the next round.

Barely a word was spoken by the team as they waited for Liam to return. Luke had briefly tried to apologise for his error that had led to the goal, but all of his teammates had quickly assured him that it wasn't his fault.

"Don't worry about it. You've probably been our best player today," said Chloe, comfortingly.

"Yeah, everyone makes mistakes, even

professionals," added Des.

Luke tried to smile, but he still felt terrible.

Alfie also felt guilty. He couldn't shake the feeling that it was his fault the Colts were struggling to qualify for the next round. He was almost certain that Madam Zola was punishing him for not heeding her advice properly.

'If only I hadn't been so quick to judge Hayden then I bet we would have already been through by now,' he said to himself.

It seemed to take ages for Jimmy and Liam to return from the organiser's table. When they eventually did reappear, Jimmy was, as ever, smiling. Liam, however, wasn't.

"We've got no chance of getting through," Liam announced miserably, as soon as he was within earshot of his teammates. "Ashgate only need a point from their final game to go through."

"Who are they playing?" all the Kingsway players asked at the same time.

"Western Dynamos," replied Liam. "Ashgate will beat them easily."

"They're not that bad. We only drew 0-0 with them," said Chloe, sounding hopeful.

"But a 0-0 draw wouldn't be any

116

good for us – we'd still go out on goal difference," answered Liam. The Colt's top goalscorer was sounding increasingly more downcast every time he spoke.

Once again, the Colts' players all went silent. None of them truly believed that Ashgate wouldn't get the point that they needed to qualify.

Eventually it was Jimmy who broke the silence. "I don't think any of you realise how fortunate you are to still be in this tournament," he said.

The Kingsway players looked startled by their coach's words.

Jimmy chuckled, realising that what he'd just said had been taken the wrong way by his players.

"I don't mean that you don't deserve to qualify. You've all worked so hard and played so well that it would be a fitting reward for you to get through to the semi-finals. What I mean is that had Rickton not scored that late penalty against Ashgate, then you'd probably already be out. Look..."

The coach took a piece of paper from his pocket and unfolded it. On it he had copied down the top of the league table. The Colts players all gathered round to look at it.

	P	W	D	L	F	A	Pts
Rickton Rovers	5	4	1	0	5	1	13
Kingsway Colts	**6**	**2**	**4**	**0**	**5**	**2**	**10**
Ashgate Athletic	5	3	0	2	8	3	9

"Do you see?" continued Jimmy. "If the Rickton and Ashgate game had finished as a draw then Rickton would have had 11 points and Ashgate would have ten – the same amount as you but with a better goal difference. That means Western Dynamos would have had to beat them by three in order for you to go through, which even I admit would have been unlikely in such a short game. But I honestly do believe they can beat them by one goal. So let's not give up just yet. We knew our fate was going to come down to other team's results whatever happened. If we get through then great, if we don't then I know you'll all be disappointed, but I'll still be proud of every single one of you. So..."

Jimmy's speech was suddenly interrupted by the sound of exaggerated clapping. "Oh good speech, old man. Very good indeed. I couldn't have said it better myself," said Keith in a mocking tone of voice. None of the Colts players or Jimmy had noticed that the North Malling coach was lurking in the background, listening to what was being said. "Not that I'd ever have to make such a speech, of course," Keith continued. "My team qualified ages ago and we've already won our group."

"Go away, Keith," snapped Jimmy. It took a lot for the old man to lose his temper, but Keith certainly seemed to have the knack of getting right under his skin.

"Oh charming," said Keith, pretending to be upset. "I was only coming over to say that I hope you lot get through and not Ashgate. They'll give us a much harder game than you lot in the semis." With that, Keith burst into a fit of hysterical laughter and walked back off in the direction of his own team.

Jimmy watched him go and then looked at this own team once more. "Look, the Ashgate vs Dynamos game starts in ten minutes on this pitch. If you do decide to watch it then I don't want any of you jeering Ashgate or trying to put their players off. That's the sort of thing he'd get you doing," the elderly coach said, gesturing towards Keith. "That's not what being a Colts player is all about."

With that Jimmy smiled again and walked off.

Alfie hadn't really been listening to Jimmy's speech and had hardly even been aware of Keith's unwanted presence. Instead, he'd been scanning the surrounding fields, looking for Hayden. He was sure that if he could befriend the boy before the match between Ashgate and Western Dynamos, then that would help the result go the way Kingsway needed it too.

After all, Madam Zola had told him he would play against Jasper at this tournament when she'd appeared on his TV screen just two days previously. Surely it was therefore his destiny to do so. Or at least it had been...

Alfie once again scolded himself for jumping to conclusions about the new boy, worried that his mistake may not only cost his team a place in the semi-final but somehow impact on his own chances of one day becoming a professional footballer as well.

He thought back to what Madam Zola had said to him through the television screen – "it's vitally important that you never judge a book by its cover. Failure to realise this could have dire consequences." He needed to prove that he had learned from his mistake and he needed to do it quickly.

Finally, Alfie spotted Hayden sitting by himself eating a sandwich. He turned and gently nudged Billy in the back. "Hey Bill, there's Hayden. Do you want to come and speak to him with me?"

Billy turned to look at his friend. "Do you not want to watch the Ashgate game? It will be on in a minute."

"I think speaking to Hayden will be more important. I mean, it's not like we can do anything about this game, is it?"

"True. But how can speaking to a boy we don't even know, and don't even like that much, be at all important?"

Alfie smiled and shook his head. "I don't know why it's important. Just that it is."

Billy frowned as he thought about what Alfie was saying. "You know what, Alf, sometimes you're really weird."

"Yep," said Alfie, happily. "So are you coming with me or not?"

"Okay I'll come. But I don't know what you expect to happen. He's even more miserable than Liam."

"We'll see," Alfie muttered, as he fixed his gaze firmly on Hayden. "We'll see."

Chapter seventeen

Alfie was thinking about what he was
actually going to say to Hayden the
entire time that he and Billy were
walking towards the other boy.

He was still unsure by the time they
had reached him.

Although the two boys stood directly in
front of Hayden, not once did the North
Malling Town player look up or even
seem aware that someone else was there.
Billy looked at Alfie and rolled his eyes
but Alfie kept his expression steady.

Finally, after 30 seconds of standing
silently in front of the newcomer, Alfie
decided it would be up to him to try and
get a conversation going. "Hi, Hayden,"
he began nervously.

Hayden didn't reply, although he did

look up and briefly raise his hand to acknowledge their presence. It wasn't much but it was a start.

"Do you mind if we sit here?" Alfie continued.

The other boy merely shrugged his shoulders, before saying very, very quietly, "If you want."

Both Alfie and Billy sat down, one on either side of Hayden. For a short while no one spoke again. Alfie didn't know what to say next so he was thankful when Billy eventually broke the uncomfortable silence.

"How do you know Keith, then?"

Hayden looked sharply at Billy. For a moment, Alfie thought that Hayden was going to get up and walk away, but then he seemed to relax a little. "I don't," he eventually replied.

"So how come you're playing for his team?" Alfie asked.

There was a short pause while Hayden considered his response. "My Mum sent an email round to all the youth teams in the Kingsway area asking if any would be interested in new players. Keith was the first person to reply."

Alfie scratched his head. He was confused. Keith only ever wanted the very best players to play for his team. How could he have possibly known that Hayden would be so good at football?

"So he'd never even seen you play before today? How did he know you were so good?"

Hayden blushed immediately, his cheeks turning a dark scarlet colour. "Well... erm... my Mum might have mentioned in the email that I was a member of Norton Town's Elite Centre."

Norton Town were a lower league professional football club located around 60 miles away from Kingsway.

"Wow, that's so cool," both Billy and

Alfie exclaimed at the same time.

"Yeah it was pretty cool," Hayden agreed. He was starting to loosen up a bit. "But my Mum says it's too far for her to keep driving me there twice a week for the training sessions. So I can't go anymore."

"You must be well gutted?" Alfie continued, desperate to keep the conversation going.

"Yeah, I only found out on Thursday night that I wouldn't be able to go again," Hayden replied sadly.

Alfie suddenly realised why Hayden had seemed so quiet at the course on Friday. As if moving to a new town hadn't been hard enough for him, he had also been told he could no longer go to an elite centre run by a professional football club. Alfie couldn't begin to imagine how horrible that must feel. "I'm really sorry about that," he said. Billy nodded his agreement.

"Still, yesterday Keith told my Mum that he might be able to get me into the Kingsway United Elite Centre with his son, so it might not be all bad," said Hayden, his mood brightening a little.

Billy and Alfie exchanged baffled glances. Only the very best players from the Kingsway area were chosen to go there. Surely there could be no way that Jasper had managed to get selected.

"Jasper's in the Kingsway United Elite Centre?" Billy asked, unable to keep the shock out of his voice.

"He's got a trial," Hayden replied, sounding equally as surprised.

Billy shook his head wildly from side to side. He simply couldn't believe that Jasper had somehow managed to get a trial for the Elite Centre. While, deep down, Billy knew that he wasn't quite as good a player as Hayden, he had no doubts that he was a far better player than Jasper. "That's so unfair," he moaned.

Alfie was also shocked to hear the news. "Are you sure?" he asked Hayden.

"Pretty sure. He showed me the letter offering him the trial when he came round our house with Keith yesterday to drop off some registration forms for next season," Hayden explained.

Billy and Alfie both shook their heads again, not quite able to take in what they were hearing. Jasper had a trial for Kingsway United! How had that happened?

Then they turned and looked at each

other as something else Hayden had just said struck them.

"Are you going to sign for North Malling Town next season?" they asked as one.

Hayden shrugged his shoulders again. "Don't know yet. Keith says that if I sign for him then he'll get me on the same trials that Jasper is on, but if I don't then he can't promise anything. So I probably will."

"How can Keith get you a trial?" Alfie asked, struggling to keep the anger out of his voice.

Once again Hayden looked unsure. "No idea. But he's got Jasper a trial, so maybe he knows someone there."

Alfie and Billy glanced at each other again. That must be it. Keith surely had a contact at the Elite Centre. All of this was just so unfair but so typical of Keith.

"What is it with you and them anyway?" Hayden continued. He was starting to sound more confident each time he spoke.

"What do you mean?" Alfie asked.

"Well, I get the feeling you don't like Keith or Jasper very much, and they certainly don't like you," said Hayden, pointing at Alfie. "All day they've been telling me how rubbish you are and that you cheat all the time, but I've watched you a couple of times today and you seem like a good player to me."

Alfie felt his cheeks go warm as he struggled to stop himself from blushing. It felt really good to hear that Hayden thought he was a good player – and it also partly explained why he had caught the other boy looking at him throughout the day.

"It's a long story..." Alfie began to say, but before he could explain any further he noticed a group of people walking towards them. Jasper and a few of his teammates.

"What are you doing with these losers?" Jasper angrily asked Hayden without so much as glancing at either Alfie or Billy.

Straight away Hayden went quiet again. He looked down at the floor and his hands automatically began picking at bits of grass. "Nothing," he answered, after a short pause.

"Good," Jasper continued. "Coz you don't want to waste your time with people that aren't any good at football. Anyway, my Dad wants to go over tactics for the semi-final against Ashgate, so come on." Jasper gestured at Hayden to get up and follow him and, reluctantly, the new boy stood and walked towards his teammates.

"We're not out yet, Jasper," said Billy. "Ashgate still might lose to Western Dynamos," he added, although he didn't honestly believe that they would.

"Did you hear something?" Jasper asked aloud. All of his teammates, except for Hayden, shook their heads. "No, thought not. Must have been the wind... or some loser trying to speak to me. Winners can't hear losers." Most of the North Malling players burst out laughing. It was as if Jasper had just told them the funniest joke they'd ever heard.

Hayden sighed sadly and walked off in the direction of Keith, swiftly followed by his giggling teammates.

"I'd love to wipe that smile off of Jasper's face," Billy seethed after the North Malling players were out of earshot. "Imagine if Ashgate lost to Dynamos and then we did manage to beat North Malling in the semi-final. Wouldn't that be amazing?"

Alfie nodded, vigorously. "It would be great," he agreed.

Both boys went silent as they spent a couple of minutes daydreaming about what it would feel like to beat North Malling Town. It was Alfie who spoke next. "Do you think Hayden actually likes playing for them?"

"Probably not," Billy answered. "But then you can't blame him for doing so. I'd do anything to get a trial for Kingsway United."

"Even play for Keith?" Alfie asked, sounding appalled.

Billy thought about it for a moment or two. "Okay, maybe not anything," he laughed. "But then we know Keith better than he does. Anyway, what are we still sitting here for? Let's go and find out how Ashgate are getting on."

Both boys stood up and turned in the direction of Pitch Three.

They were about to run back to their friends when they noticed something which immediately stopped them in their tracks. Even from where they were standing the two friends could see that some of the players on the pitch were celebrating wildly together.

Ashgate Athletic had just scored a goal!

Chapter eighteen

The rest of the Colts players looked absolutely devastated as Alfie and Billy approached them.

"I take it Ashgate are winning?" a glum sounding Billy asked his teammates.

To his and Alfie's surprise, though, Liam shook his head. "No they've just scored to make it 1-1. Dynamos scored really early on but Ashgate have been all over them ever since."

"The game must be nearly over as well," added Chloe the moment Liam had stopped talking. "The second half seems to be going on for ages. We're definitely not going to get through."

"The game's not over until the final whistle blows," said Jimmy, calmly. "It only takes a second to score a goal." The elderly coach smiled warmly at every single one of his players. "And anyway, does it really matter if we don't get through? As long as we've all had fun today, that's the most important thing."

The Kingsway players barely grunted in response. Although they all realised that playing for enjoyment was more important than playing to win, they were desperate to get through just so that they could have the opportunity to beat Keith and Jasper's team in the semi-final. They would simply be gutted if they were knocked out now.

In the distance, Alfie could see Keith talking to his team. As usual, Hayden was sitting a little way apart from his teammates, who were all huddled close to Keith, hanging on his every word.

'He'd be much happier playing for us,' Alfie mused. Since spending a little bit of time with the new boy he had quickly grown to like him. Once again Madam Zola had been right. Hayden was alright. Alfie had badly misjudged him.

Alfie's attention was quickly brought back to the game going on in front of him by a sudden scream from his friends.

"GO ON!" the Colts players shouted together as the Dynamos striker went through one on one with the Ashgate goalkeeper.

All of the Kingsway players rose to their feet as they waited to see what the Dynamos striker would do.

"Shoot," bellowed Liam.

"Take it round him," suggested Billy.

"Just please score," pleaded Chloe.

The Dynamos striker looked up at the goal. He could hear some people on the sideline urging him to shoot, others telling him to take the ball around the goalkeeper. In fact, so many different instructions were being shouted that the poor boy just didn't know what to do for the best.

As he struggled to make up his mind, the Ashgate goalkeeper raced off of his goal line and, taking full advantage of the Dynamos' player's indecision, smuggled the ball away from the striker and grasped it gratefully into his chest.

The chance was gone and with it surely the Colts' hopes of qualifying for the semi-finals. There was a collective groan from all the Kingsway players as Ashgate's goalie stood up with the ball safely in his hands.

The goalkeeper took the ball to the very edge of his area and then cleared it upfield, kicking it as far as he possibly could. The ball crossed the halfway line and then bounced just in front of one of the Dynamos' defenders. The defender swung his foot at the ball, not really worried about where it landed just so long as he got it away from the danger zone.

However, to his, and everyone else's astonishment the ball flew high up in the air and headed towards the Ashgate goal. The goalkeeper was still standing way off his line and could only watch as the ball sailed over him and towards the goal. As he tried to scramble desperately back to his line he slipped and the ball landed inches from his hands and began bouncing towards the line.

The Kingsway players felt like they were watching a slow motion replay on the television as they watched the ball trickle towards the line. It seemed to be taking ages to go in. The unfortunate Ashgate 'keeper made one more last-gasp attempt to claw the ball away from the goalline.

But he was too late.

Finally the ball crossed the line.

Dynamos had scored!

There was a second of complete silence

as the Kingsway players digested what had just happened. Then, as one, they all whooped aloud and began cheering at the top of their voices.

They were cheering so loudly that they didn't even notice the referee bring the game to a close barely 30 seconds later. In the end, Jimmy had to order his players to stop celebrating and go and offer their sympathies to the Ashgate players. After all, they had let in three last minute goals in consecutive games and it had cost them their place in the semi-finals. Their players were understandably dismayed.

However, while they did feel sorry for the unlucky Ashgate Athletic players, Alfie and his teammates were finding it extremely hard to keep the smiles from their faces.

Against all odds, the Kingsway Colts had qualified as group runners up and would now play North Malling Town in the semi-final.

Chapter nineteen

Keith looked shocked as he watched the Kingsway players make their way over to Pitch Two, where the semi-final was to be played.

He had been certain that his old team would not make it out of their group and he'd not been quite able to believe his eyes when he saw that it was the parents of the Ashgate Athletic players who were packing their belongings away, not Kingsway's.

The truth was that, for all of Keith's bragging and showboating, he really hadn't wanted to play the Colts. Not today anyway. This was the first time his new team had ever played together and while he knew that North Malling Town certainly had the better players, he couldn't deny that Kingsway had a great team spirit. Even Keith realised that sometimes this was as important as ability. Only sometimes, though.

Keith flushed as he felt his heart begin to pound in his chest. There was no way he could let his old team beat his new team. He couldn't be shown up by them. Not again. Keith's pride was still wounded from Alfie's victory over Jasper many months earlier. He couldn't possibly let the Colts get one over on him a second time.

Keith looked over to where his team were playing keep ball as part of a warm up exercise. He smiled menacingly as he saw Hayden confidently flick the ball away from a player who was trying to get the ball off him, and then back heel it straight to Jasper's feet. He started to relax. With Hayden in his team there was no way North Malling could lose.

The Kingsway Colts' players had also seen Hayden's sublime bit of skill. "He's certainly a special player," said Jimmy, admiration pouring from his voice.

None of the Colts players said anything. They all looked in awe of the boy. Every single one of them was thinking the same thing; 'how can we possibly beat North

Malling with Hayden on their team?'

Jimmy had already told his players what the team for the semi-final would be. It was a tough decision as every outfield player had already had a turn at being sub, so this would mean that one player would have missed one game more than the others.

Jimmy hated to be unfair, but he had to make a choice and in the end Des was the unlucky boy to be left out. The elderly coach was pleased that, despite being obviously disappointed, Des accepted the decision without grumbling too much and wished his friends the best of luck.

Luke had been surprised to be named in the starting line-up. He knew he wasn't as good at football as his teammates, but Jimmy echoed some of his own player's earlier words when he told the young defender that he had been one of the Colts' best players that day.

Shortly before the stated kick off time, Jimmy called his players in for a quick team talk, just as Keith did the same for North Malling.

The players on both teams got into a huddle around their coach, but none of the boys or Chloe were really taking in what they were being told by their respective coaches. They were all too nervous about the game ahead to be able to concentrate properly.

After a short while, the referee blew his whistle to bring the captains of both teams into the middle of the pitch for the coin toss.

Jasper strode confidently to the halfway line in complete contrast to the Colts' captain, Danny, who shuffled nervously towards his former teammate.

Although Danny may have been the Colts' tallest player, he was still dwarfed by Jasper, who looked more like an under 12s player than he did a boy who was just about to step up to the under 10s.

The referee tossed the coin. Jasper correctly called heads and chose to kick off. "Good luck," said Danny, tentatively holding out his hand for Jasper to shake.

Jasper ignored the outstretched hand. "You're the ones who are going to need luck," he sneered.

The ref looked sharply at Jasper, to which the North Malling captain merely shrugged his shoulders and innocently stated that he was joking and that he and Danny were old friends. Danny didn't smile. Neither did the ref.

While the coin toss had been taking

place, Alfie had rushed over to his bag, telling his friends that he needed to check on something quickly. He felt around in his bag until he could feel the teddy bear that Madam Zola had given him as a present shortly before Christmas.

'Come on Madam Zola,' he said quietly to himself. 'Please help me to beat Jasper again. I'm really sorry I didn't listen to you. I promise I'll never ignore what you tell me ever again.' With that he removed his hand from the bag, zipped it up and ran onto the pitch.

As Alfie went to stand in his right midfield position he ran past Hayden. The two boys shared a quick smile with each other. Hayden looked as though he was just about to say something, but then he noticed Jasper glaring at him so decided it would probably be best not to say anything at all. He quickly moved his eyes away from Alfie's.

Seconds later the shrill sound of the referee's whistle got the semi-final underway.

From the kick-off, Liam passed the ball to Billy who in turn played it out wide to Alfie. However, almost before he even had the ball under control he felt his legs taken from underneath him and he hit the ground with a thud. Alfie didn't even need to look up to know Jasper had been responsible for the foul. Less than ten seconds had been played and already Alfie had a feeling that he wasn't going to enjoy this game very much.

"Sorry ref," Jasper apologised immediately, sounding every bit as insincere as he felt. "He was just too quick for me."

"No more!" replied the ref. He had already taken a disliking to Jasper following the coin toss incident.

The opening minutes of the game were stop-start, with neither team able to gain any real control of the match. Hayden had hardly had the ball at his feet as his teammates seemed far more intent on kicking Kingsway's players than they did on actually playing football. The only other North Malling player who had yet to give a foul away was the boy Danny had spoken to earlier in the day – although even he had taken a couple of wild swipes at Billy that the Colts' player had just about managed to evade.

Every time the ref awarded Kingsway a foul, all of the Colts' parents made clear their disgust at the tackles their children were being subjected to. Keith, meanwhile, continually protested his team's innocence, bellowing at the top of his voice that the ref was being too soft and that football was fast becoming a "non-contact sport."

Jimmy was doing his best to remain calm. He urged his team's parents to do the same. The last thing he wanted was Kingsway involved in a battle off the pitch as well as on it.

With half-time approaching, North Malling looked as if they had finally got bored with repeatedly kicking their opponents and had actually started to play some really good football. For most of the half, Danny and Luke had managed to keep Hayden quiet and as a result Pranav had not yet had a save to make. At the other end, Billy and Liam had both had shots on target, but they were dealt with quite easily by North Malling's goalkeeper.

However, now that North Malling had started to pass the ball around they had taken control of the game and they looked like a very good footballing side.

Even Jasper was much improved from the player he had been at the Colts, although he was still one of his team's weakest players.

Following a really good passing move by North Malling, Hayden got the ball in space for the first time in the match. Before the Colts players even had a chance to blink he had jinked his way skilfully past Chloe and Danny. Luke rushed over to make a tackle but before he could get to him, Hayden had played a wonder pass with the outside of his left boot, steering the ball right into the path of a teammate. The North Malling midfielder had plenty of time to pick his spot and rammed the ball hard and low past Pranav. North Malling led 1-0.

"Yessss! Get in there," screamed Keith at the top of his voice as he pumped both of his fists in the air. "Now let's show these losers how to play football!"

Hayden didn't join in his team's manic celebrations. Instead he chose to make his way back to his position, ready to restart the game – a fact that had been noted by an over excited Jasper, who was charging around like he'd just won the World Cup all by himself.

Less than a minute later, the half-time whistle sounded.

As the players made their way off the pitch, Jasper ran over to confront Hayden.

"What's wrong with you?" he shouted at his teammate, his round face going red with rage. "We're winning 1-0 in a semi-final and you still can't even be bothered to celebrate with us. Do you even care that we're winning?"

Hayden looked stunned. "I... er... I... Just want to play football," he said, struggling to get the words out.

"Well buck your ideas up. We need to beat these muppets. And beat them by loads!"

Hayden didn't know what to say, so he just carried on walking towards Keith, ignoring his captain who was still yelling at him at the top of his voice.

He'd scored most of the team's goals during the tournament so far and just set up the goal that had given them the lead in the semi-final. What was Jasper's problem?

Jasper's outburst had been witnessed by Jimmy and all of the Colts players – all of whom looked as surprised as Hayden did.

Even Keith shot Jasper an angry look as his son walked towards him. The last thing he wanted was for Jasper to upset the team's star player.

"What was that all about?" Alfie asked as he and his teammates gathered

144

around Jimmy to listen to his half-time team talk.

"I've got no idea," replied Jimmy. "But let's forget about it for a minute. We need to concentrate on the second half. Now listen up..."

As Jimmy gave his team talk, Alfie glanced towards Hayden. It looked as though Keith was making Jasper apologise to him and after a few moments the two North Malling Town players begrudgingly shook hands. Neither Jasper nor Hayden looked particularly happy about it, though.

North Malling's players were already back on the pitch by the time Jimmy had finished talking. The Kingsway coach had been unusually passionate in addressing his team and had urged them to wipe the smile off Keith's face once and for all.

The Kingsway players had never heard Jimmy so animated and were clearly fired up as they retook to the pitch for the second half. They were determined to give it everything they had in an attempt to turn the match around.

Jimmy just hoped that sheer determination and effort would be enough.

Chapter twenty

Jasper was still furious as he waited for the second half to begin. He was standing in his central midfield position, scowling at the back of Hayden's head.

There were many things that Jasper was finding not to like about the new boy.

Firstly, Hayden had hardly said two words to any of the North Malling players all day long. Yet he seemed to have made friends with Alfie. 'Why would anyone want to be friends with that little muppet when they could be friends with me?' Jasper whined to himself.

The North Malling Town captain also didn't like the fact that Hayden hadn't once joined in celebrating a goal – even though he had scored most of the team's goals himself.

But worst of all, although he would
never admit it out loud, Jasper hated the
way his own Dad acted towards Hayden.
Anyone would have thought that the
newcomer was the best football player
in the world the way Keith carried on
around him. He could not believe that his
Dad had promised to get Hayden a trial
for the Kingsway United Elite Centre.
Jasper wanted to be the only person to
have that honour in his team. 'It's almost
like he thinks Hayden's a better player
than me,' he said to himself angrily.

And, to top it all off, Keith had then
humiliated Jasper by forcing him to
apologise to Hayden in front of all his
teammates during the half-time break.
Keith was cross with him and Jasper
couldn't remember the last time he'd been
on the end of one of his father's tempers.
He hoped he wouldn't be again anytime
soon.

As Kingsway's players came back onto
the pitch, Jasper once again saw Alfie
and Hayden acknowledge each other.
Jasper's blood boiled, but he knew he had
to control his temper. For now at least.

North Malling got the second half
underway and straight from the restart
they went on the attack. Hayden was

at the centre of everything, causing the Kingsway defence constant problems with his intelligent running and awesome ball skills. No matter how hard they tried, Luke and Danny simply couldn't get near him.

Kingsway were hanging on as North Malling launched wave after wave of attack. Only a combination of wasteful finishing from North Malling, some good saves from Pranav, and the crossbar kept the Colts within one goal of their opponents.

"We need to get Billy on the ball more," shouted Jimmy. It was unusual for the elderly coach to single out one of his players, but it was no secret that Billy was his team's best player and at that moment they needed him on the ball if they were to stand any chance of reaching the final.

Not long after Jimmy had given the command, Kingsway finally managed to get the ball to Billy's feet for the first time in the second half.

Straight away, Billy darted towards the North Malling goal, keen to show that Hayden wasn't the only boy who possessed great skills.

He used his electrifying speed to tear

past the Malling midfielders and then feinted to pass to Liam. The defenders fell for the trick and Billy dropped his shoulder to sail past them with ease. He reached the edge of the area before curling a superb shot towards the far corner.

For a moment it looked as if the ball was going to nestle in the bottom corner of the net, but instead it rolled agonisingly inches wide of the target.

"That's more like it," shouted Jimmy encouragingly. "Keep the effort going Colts."

Keith was not happy. "You do not let him beat any of you that easily again! Understand," he roared. His players nodded. Jasper smiled wickedly.

Kingsway were clearly feeling buoyed by Billy's near miss. Suddenly it was their turn to attack. Alfie and Chloe combined well on the right wing and Liam was not too far away from getting on the end of Chloe's deep cross.

Liam then tried to play a through ball to Alfie, but he slightly over hit his pass and it just about rolled safely through to the opposition's goalkeeper.

With time running out, and Kingsway still doing most of the attacking, North

Malling had started to resort back to their earlier tactics of fouling Kingsway's players. To Keith's obvious delight, his team were being very careful about where they were giving free kicks away, making sure they were not in positions where the Colts could shoot from.

Although Jimmy was not at all surprised to see Keith applauding such tactics, he couldn't stop himself from glaring angrily at his counterpart. "It's all part of the game, old man," beamed Keith. "It's called playing to win." Jimmy just shook his head in disbelief.

There were now just seconds of the semi-final remaining. As Danny picked himself off the ground following yet another cynical tackle from a North Malling player, Billy ran over to take the free kick. "Quickly, Danny. Tap the ball to me while they're not looking," he urged his teammate.

Danny did as he was told and Billy immediately set off on another run up the field. The North Malling players hadn't even realised that the Colts had taken a quick free kick, and it was only Keith's panicked screaming that alerted them to what had happened.

Billy was bearing down on the North

150

Malling goal at speed when, from out of nowhere, Jasper threw himself at the winger shoulder first, wiping his opponent clean out. Billy crumpled to the floor, his pain clear for all to see. Mr Morris rushed quickly onto the pitch. "Are you going to do something about that ref?" he cried, before going over to check on his wounded son.

The ref walked over to Keith. "I demand you sub that boy off right this minute," he ordered the North Malling coach.

"But we don't have any subs..."

"Then you'll have to play with six players for the little time that remains. I

am not having deliberate acts of fouling like that on my pitch!"

Keith was just about to argue with the ref, but the official had already walked off, his decision made. Keith sighed to himself. "Jasper come over here, now," he called.

"Am I being sent off?" Jasper asked in a way that sounded as though being shown a red card would be something to be proud of.

"Not exactly," replied Keith. "Just another example of football becoming a non-contact sport." He said this just loud enough for Jimmy to hear, but before the Kingsway coach could react, Keith turned his back on the old man and walked up to the other end of the pitch.

Billy was too badly hurt to continue. "I'm going to take him to hospital, just as a precaution," said Mr Morris as he carried his son off of the pitch. "Can someone take Alfie home for me, please?"

Chloe's Mum said she would and all of the people involved with Kingsway clapped as Billy was carried towards his Dad's car.

Back on the pitch, the Colts had a free kick in a dangerous position. Alfie was standing over the ball. With the usual free-kick taker Billy off the pitch and on his way to hospital, Alfie knew that this was his chance. His moment of glory.

A goal here and the match would surely go into extra time. And playing with a man advantage, he was sure the Colts could – and indeed would – go on to win the game. Alfie stared at the top right hand corner of the goal. He visualised the ball hitting the net as he waited patiently for the ref to blow his whistle.

The whistle sounded.

Alfie began his run-up.

He connected perfectly with the ball sending it over the North Malling wall and heading straight for the top corner of the net.

Just as in the previous game, when the Colts had waited for the Dynamos' winning goal to cross the line, time seemed to slow down.

The ball glided through the air, exactly as Alfie had intended it to do. North Malling's goalkeeper didn't move. He knew he was beaten.

Alfie raised his right arm aloft ready to celebrate.

And then time suddenly seemed to speed up again as the ball smashed against the crossbar and bounced harmlessly out of play.

Alfie couldn't believe it. Nor could his teammates or the watching parents. He had been so close.

The final whistle sounded the moment the North Malling goalie took the resulting goal kick.

Kingsway were out. North Malling had won.

Keith and Jasper went wild with delight, running onto the pitch screaming at the top of their voices. All of the North Malling players, aside from Hayden, joined hands and danced around in a circle. Judging from the look on Hayden's face you would have thought he'd been on the losing team, not the winning one.

The Colts' players were almost inconsolable. All seven of them were trying their best not to cry, but all of them had tears welling up in the corners of their eyes.

Jimmy somehow managed to look gutted and proud all at the same time, but no matter how many times he told his players how pleased with them he was, he just couldn't make them feel any better.

Just then, Keith swaggered over to the Colts. "Bad luck boys," he said. For a moment he sounded like he meant it. "But when you're losers, you're losers," he quickly added in his familiar mocking tone.

Jimmy was just about to react angrily to the bully when he noticed Hayden walking towards them.

"Can I go home with you, Alfie?" he asked.

Keith smiled. "It's not time to go yet, superstar. We've got a final to play. Come on, let's go and get ready."

Keith began walking off, but Hayden stayed standing right where he was. "Come on Hayden this is no time for games," called Keith, starting to sound concerned.

"I don't want to play for your team anymore. I want to play for the Colts."

Keith looked stunned. And not just because this was the longest sentence he'd ever heard Hayden say. "You... you... you... want to play... for these... losers," Keith spluttered, just about managing to spit out the last word. He had gone so red in the face that it looked as though he would explode at any moment.

Hayden shrugged his shoulders. "Yeah," he replied, simply.

"But... what about your Kingsway

United trial?... I told you I'd only sort that for you if you signed for us."

Hayden shrugged again but stayed silent.

Keith shook his head in disbelief.

"You see, Keith," said Jimmy, grinning from ear to ear. "I told you there was more to football than winning."

Hayden nodded. "I just want to enjoy myself," he said.

Keith sighed loudly and stormed back in the direction of his team, trying to work out how he could explain to them that they'd be one person short for the final.

Hayden turned to face his new teammates. They had suddenly forgotten all about losing against North Malling and were now all smiling as widely as their coach.

"Welcome to the Colts, lad," said Jimmy. "It's great to have you here."

Chapter twenty one

After much pleading from Alfie and Chloe, Mrs Reed eventually agreed to stop off at the hospital on their way home so that they could check in on Billy and tell him about what had happened.

Hayden was sitting inbetween the two friends in the car. He told Chloe and her Mum all about how he had ended up playing for Keith's team, and about the Norton Town Elite Centre.

"Oh, so that's why you were so miserable on Friday at the course," said Chloe, once Hayden had finished telling his story.

Alfie shot Chloe a warning glance. He didn't want anyone to upset him again.

Chloe began to apologise, but Hayden merely laughed. "That's alright. I was being a bit of a... idiot, I guess. I'm just shy."

"That's alright," said Alfie. "So am I."

When they got to the hospital it didn't take them long to locate Billy in the accident and emergency ward. He was sitting up in a bed with his Dad by his side. He eyed Hayden suspiciously, but said nothing.

"How you doing, Bill?" Alfie asked the second he was close enough to his friend to speak.

"Alright I suppose. I've got a cracked rib and a mild... conclusion?"

"Concussion, Billy," said Mr Morris with a smile. "It's a mild concussion."

"Whatever. Anyway, I've got to stay in here overnight but I should be allowed to go home in the morning and I should be able to play football again by the start of next season." Billy looked at Hayden. "So what actually happened in the match? Did we win?"

Alfie and Chloe began to excitedly describe the events that had just taken place and when they had finished their tale both Billy and his Dad laughed out loud.

"I wish I could have seen Keith's face," said Mr Morris, inbetween bouts of laughter. "I bet it was a real picture."

It was then Hayden's turn to ask his new friends about why they didn't like Keith or Jasper. It took quite a long time for everyone to explain the whole story to him but, by the time they had finished, Hayden knew that he had made the right choice to become a Kingsway player.

"I doubt we've seen the last of Keith or Jasper just yet, though," said Mrs Reed, ominously. "North Malling are bound to be in our league next season."

Everyone agreed. Then Mrs Reed insisted that they should get going as she still had to get both Alfie and Hayden home. The group said their goodbyes and were just making their way towards the exit when Liam came running into the room.

"Hi Bill, hi guys," he shouted excitedly as his parents trundled into the room behind him. "You should have stayed right till the end of the tournament," he continued, barely able to catch his breath. "North Malling got thrashed in the final by Rickton Rovers, 4-0! Keith and Jasper were really angry. It was so funny. They are not happy with you or you, though," Liam laughed, pointing first at Hayden, then at Alfie.

"What did I do?" Alfie asked, genuinely confused.

"Jasper seems to think you stole Hayden off them by telling lies about him throughout the day."

Alfie shrugged. "Whatever. Let's face it, it's not exactly the first time that Jasper's been out to get me, is it?"

Everyone laughed again. "Stop making me laugh," pleaded Billy. "It really hurts my ribs."

"Come on you three. Let's get going," said Mrs Reed again.

Alfie went and gave his best friend a gentle high-five before saying goodbye. As he turned to leave, for the third time that day he bumped into a table, scattering the contents all over the floor.

"Sorry," he exclaimed, before bending down to pick up the fallen objects. One item caught his attention straight away. It was a pen that looked exactly like the ones he had knocked over outside the tent at the tournament.

"Where did you get this?" he asked Mr Morris.

"Funnily enough it was tucked under one of my windscreen wipers when we got back to our car," replied Billy's Dad. "You can keep it if you like."

Alfie said that he would very much like to keep it, although he didn't really know what he wanted a pen for.

He thanked Mr Morris for the gift before following the other three out the door.

Back in Chloe's Mum's car, Alfie was fiddling with his new pen and daydreaming when he suddenly noticed something that he hadn't seen before. There was some writing on the pen.

Alfie held the pen closer to his eyes so that he could read what it said.

He smiled to himself.

On the pen were two letters. Initials. 'MZ'.

Alfie couldn't help but feel that he was still on track to fulfil his destiny.

Kingsway Colts' group results and league table

ROUND 1
KINGSWAY COLTS 1 RICKTON ROVERS 1
Ashgate Athletic 2 Heath Hill United 0
Southfield United 0 Western Dynamos 0

ROUND 2
KINGSWAY COLTS 0 WESTERN DYNAMOS 0
Lakeland Spurs 1 Ashgate Athletic 3
Heath Hill United 0 Southfield United 1

ROUND 3
KINGSWAY COLTS 0 HEATH HILL UNITED 0
Southfield United 0 Lakeland Spurs 0
Rickton Rovers 1 Western Dynamos 0

ROUND 4
KINGSWAY COLTS 2 LAKELAND SPURS 0
Rickton Rovers 1 Heath Hill United 0
Southfield United 0 Ashgate Athletic 3

ROUND 5
KINGSWAY COLTS 1 ASHGATE ATHLETIC 0
Western Dynamos 0 Heath Hill United 1
Lakeland Spurs 0 Rickton Rovers 1

ROUND 6
KINGSWAY COLTS 1 SOUTHFIELD UNITED 1
Ashgate Athletic 0 Rickton Rovers 1
Western Dynamos 1 Lakeland Spurs 2

ROUND 7
Lakeland Spurs 0 Heath Hill United 1
Southfield United 0 Rickton Rovers 2
Ashgate Athletic 1 Western Dynamos 2

	P	W	D	L	F	A	Pts
Rickton Rovers	6	5	1	0	7	1	16
Kingsway Colts	**6**	**2**	**4**	**0**	**5**	**2**	**10**
Ashgate Athletic	6	3	0	3	9	5	9
Heath Hill United	6	2	1	3	2	4	7
Southfield United	6	1	3	2	2	6	6
Western Dynamos	6	1	2	3	3	5	5
Lakeland Spurs	6	1	1	3	3	8	4

Turn the page to read the opening chapter of **Split Loyalties** *- a Kindle only book written by David Fuller.*

Download your copy today...

Hugh

Hugh Capulet had been completely
obsessed with football for as long as he
– or anyone else for that matter – could
remember.

From the very moment that Hugh had
taken his first unsteady steps at just over
ten-months old, a ball had rarely been far
from his feet.

As a baby, he would simply refuse point
blank to fall asleep unless a football
was placed in his cot, while few, if any,
childhood photos of Hugh exist in which
he's not either kicking or dribbling a ball.

In fact, there is probably more chance of
seeing a photo of the Loch Ness Monster
and Bigfoot sitting together whilst
enjoying a quiet cup of tea on the lawns
of Buckingham Palace, than there is of

seeing a picture of an adolescent Hugh without a ball somewhere near his feet.

Given the extent of his obsession, it's probably not all that surprising to learn that Hugh began to exhibit a talent for the sport before he was even out of nappies. He was as comfortable dribbling a football as most babies are dribbling their dinner down their clothes.

By the age of nine, Hugh had been selected for League One Portland Town's Academy team. He signed his first professional contract with the same club on his seventeenth birthday, having won the team's player of the year award every single season since first joining the academy.

It didn't take long for Premier League scouts to recognise Hugh's obvious potential. Whilst still a teenager he signed his first multi-million pound contract with the newly-crowned league champions, Lexington Albion – England's most successful ever football team.

Since then, a raft of individual and team honours had come his way and he had even become a regular for the Italian national team.

Yet, in spite of all the trophies that he'd won, the fan adulation he'd received, and the massive amounts of money he had earned in the seven years since first signing for Lexington, it was still a love of football, rather than any other associated reward, that made him tick.

Each and every time he stepped onto a pitch, he still received the exact same buzz that he had experienced before playing his very first match as a six year old for the Ashgate Athletic under 7s.

His heart beat would start to race and a nervous shiver of excitement would run down the entire length of his spine. An involuntary beaming smile would then break out across his face.

For years he had tended to be the first player to arrive at Lexington's luxurious Middleton training complex every single day, and more often than not he would be the last to leave, too.

And when he wasn't playing in a match or at training, the chances were that he was either watching a match on the TV, or playing one of his many football-related console games.

Yes, it's fair to say that Hugh Capulet had been completely obsessed with football for a very, very long time.

Until now.

There was just one day remaining

before Hugh was due to meet up with his Italian teammates ahead of boarding a plane to travel to Brazil for the World Cup and Hugh should have been buzzing with excitement. This was due to be his first major international tournament, having picked up a tournament-ending knee injury on the eve of the European Championships two years earlier.

Feeling fit and healthy, and having just had the best season of his career with Lexington, he should have been looking forward to the prospect of playing in the biggest football tournament of all. He should have been as excited as a hyperactive four-year-old on Christmas Eve.

Instead he was dreading it.

And it was all his family's fault.

Visit the Kindle store today to read the rest of Split Loyalties

STEP INTO MY POWER

JAMIA
WILSON

ANDREA
PIPPINS

WIDE EYED EDITIONS

CONTENTS

POWER

COMMUNITY

CHOICES

INTRODUCTION

Do you remember a time when you felt powerful?

Illustrator Andrea Pippins remembers stepping into her power when she ran for the role of sixth-grade class president and won. She felt like her ideas and voice mattered when she heard her classmates' interests for the school year and wove them, along with her vision, into a campaign and community events.

Similarly, I felt powerful when I had opportunities to speak my truth during my youth. I'll never forget the sense of purpose I felt when I was first asked to recite my poetry at a church conference. I reflect on this moment when I need a reminder that my voice is, and always has been, a megaphone that I use to change hearts and minds, and advocate for justice.

Both Andrea and I know first-hand that learning how to own and use our power as girls and young women helped us realise our dreams. We understand that the world can be tough to navigate at every level, from handling conflicts with friends, family members and bullies, to dealing with politics, inequality, sickness, hardships and having to obey rules you inherited or aren't old enough to vote for or against.

That's why we'll be exploring what it means to know and trust our insights and capabilities with stories, images, activities, resources and action prompts that you can interact with on your own time and, most importantly, on your terms. No matter where you are, *Step into My Power* is here for you with caring advice and actions you can take and make your very own. It's an invitation to take steps, big leaps or small tip-toes towards your goals. This book is a celebration of the fact that you are entirely enough as you are, but might need encouragement while reaching for your goals. It's here to be your unconditionally loving friend or even an imaginary sibling if you're an only child like we are.

You are not alone, even if it feels that way sometimes. Think of this book as a paper-bound sat-nav that can help you navigate your thoughts and feelings. Whether times are joyful, rough or somewhere in between, *Step into My Power* will always have your back. Although you already possess all you need inside of you, we are here to reassure you every day, every week and every month that you are enough, and you have what it takes to turn your vision for your life into action.

Jamia Wilson & Andrea Pippins

YOU'VE

tap into your strengths

HAVE YOU EVER FELT LIKE YOU'RE NOT SURE WHAT YOU'RE GOOD AT, OR THAT THE THINGS YOU DO WELL DON'T MATTER AS MUCH AS THE WAYS OTHER PEOPLE SHINE?

When I was younger, I used to feel that way. I wasn't an expert ballerina or award-winning swimmer, like some of my friends, and I was in a school that valued physical achievement.

I didn't see my unique gifts as assets when I was growing up. Teachers and parents made me feel bad about things they prioritised, such as being a whiz at algebra, and playing tennis (which flared up my asthma and ignited my anxiety). I sulked about not fitting into the mould people in charge expected of an otherwise 'good' student.

GOT THIS!

Instead of embracing my talents, I quietly beat myself up for not being a perfect child who was skilled at everything I tried. Whenever my father or a teacher would say, "But you're so smart, you are not working up to your potential in maths, or Arabic class, or 'fill-in-the-blank with something I'm not a genius about'", my breath became shallow. I knew deep inside that I learned differently when it came to numbers, and although I wasn't as quick at maths, my talent for word problems in the same maths class would later help me achieve my dreams as a writer when I grew up.

I share this story because I walked around with a secret for many years. I hid behind my sunny smile and felt ashamed that I had to have a tutor to help me with Mathematics, due to my visual disability and the challenges that came with it.

INSTEAD OF FORCING MYSELF TO BE SOMEONE ELSE'S BEST SELF, I'D WRITE MY YOUNGER SELF THIS LETTER ON MY FAVORITE STATIONERY:

Mia,

The world would be boring if we were all good at the same things. Don't beat yourself up for not being perfect. Take time to listen and hear what people ask you for help on, and compliment

you about. What aspects of who you are, are you most proud of? What do folks appreciate about what you share with them, and most of all what stirs your soul so much that you never look at your watch when you're doing it – because therein lies your answer – and follow it.

Love,
Your Older Self

P. S. Oh, and… Keep reading and writing. It will help you find your purpose.

➤ STEP INTO YOUR POWER

Imagine you are older;
write a love letter to yourself
right now...

Speak to yourself with the
same gentle and generous
spirit you would use to address
a very small child.

Pay attention to the courageous
whispers from your heart, and
less to the roar of critique from
the world around you.

You are impacting the world
in your own special way.

Recognise your natural
abilities and passions and
urge yourself to keep going
with them – even if not
everyone values them with
the same weight you do.

Although I'd love to meet the small percentage of humans who have never experienced dread or angst at some point in their life, the reality is that most of us are – or have been – afraid of something.

As someone whose family once nicknamed her 'worry wart', it can be challenging to confess my fears to people who might judge the things that stir me up – like the stage fright I still experience every time I speak in public (even though I do it often, and for a living). But I'm facing my fears and calling on you to join me. Let's get to know your concerns, understand their roots and end our shame so we can share our unique gifts with the world.

Once I learned that our amygdala (the fear centre of the brain), is triggered whenever we feel something is threatening, it helped me make sense of whether this small, two-centimetre region of our brain is telling me the truth, or making a mountain out of a molehill.

This 'fight or flight' response can be useful when there's a hungry tiger chasing us down the street – it makes us panic and run! But things like performing in a school talent show can set off similar spinning thoughts, restless legs, sweaty palms, feelings of doom or however it personally shows up for you. These physical responses can make the two feel eerily similar.

THAT'S WHY I'M SHARING SOME OF THE TIPS I'VE USED ALONG THE WAY THAT HELP ME SLAY THE FEAR-TIGER THAT TRIES TO CHASE ME DOWN EVERY TIME I MOVE TOWARDS BEING BRAVE.

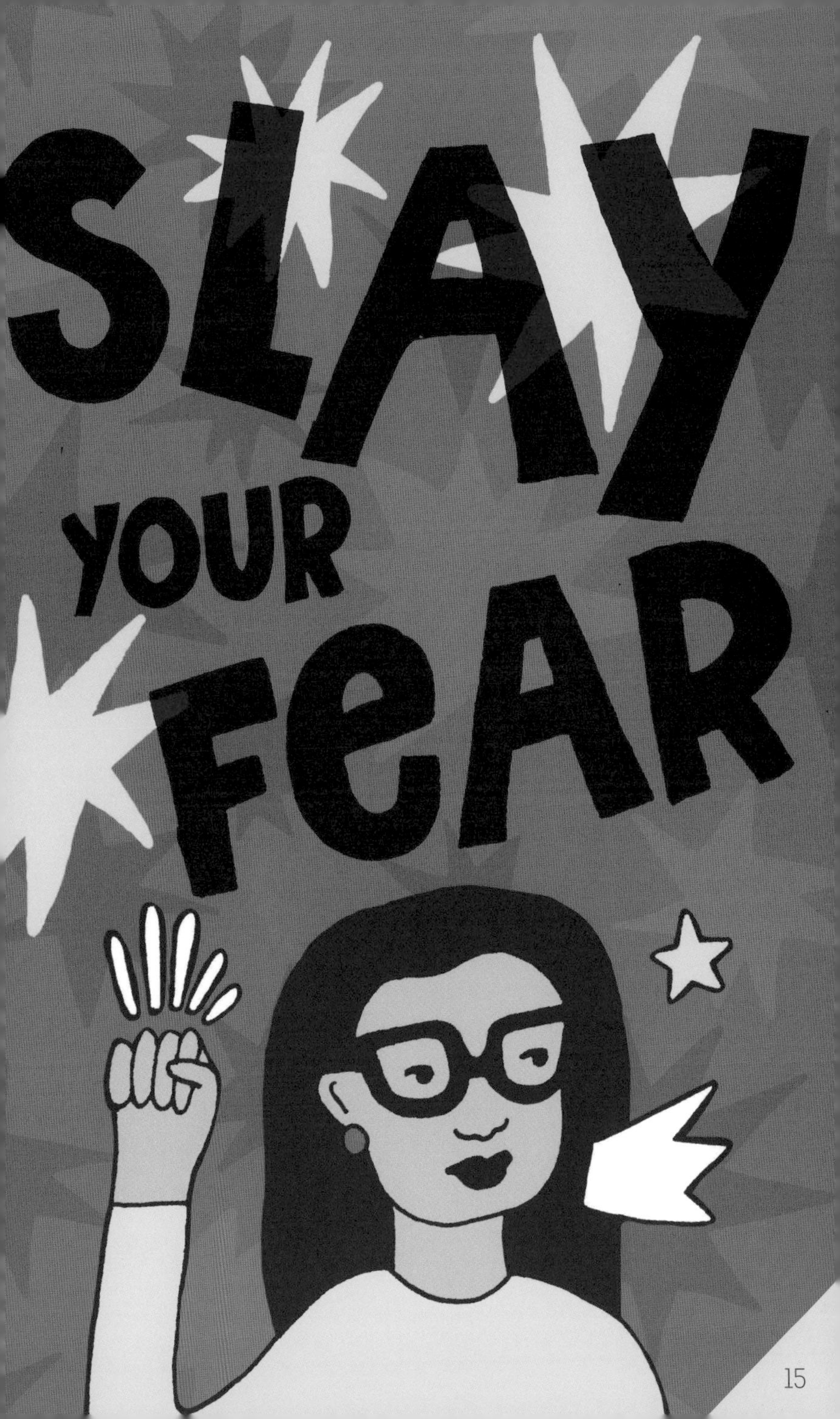
SLAY
YOUR
FEAR

▶ STEP INTO YOUR POWER

FIRST, INTRODUCE ME TO YOUR FRENEMY, FEAR.

Make a name tag for Fear. Write down who they are, where they are from, where you first met them, and what they look, smell and sound like. Sketch them out on a piece of paper. If your Fear is a shadowy shape-shifter, make a list of all of their alter-egos and aliases. Once you write them down, thank Fear for all you've learned from them and then ceremoniously bid them farewell by ripping up the paper.

Now that you've taken a courageous step, it's time to make another one. Former American First Lady Eleanor Roosevelt once said,

"You gain strength, courage and confidence by every experience in which you stop to look fear in the face."

Her words are often misattributed to say 'do one thing that scares you every day', which I took to heart and added to my calendar as a daily prompt. When I wake up, I write down 'today's bold move' in my calendar every day. Depending on the day it varies from 'be honest about your need for solitude or space' to 'go to a group class at the gym' (which brings this bookworm back to panic about having to play mandatory team sports in high school).

What's your bold move today or this week? **DO IT. I DARE YOU.**

TELL THE TRUTH:

"WHAT'S THE WORST THING THAT CAN HAPPEN?"

is a question I've learned to ask myself when I struggle with simply saying one powerful two-letter word, 'no'. In almost every instance, the reality of what might happen if I set a boundary that is healthy, is not as terrible as the cost of not being true to myself.

One of my first memories of my battle with 'no' occurred when my Grandma asked all of my girl cousins to help wash Christmas dinner dishes, while our male cousins were allowed to play games. As a spunky seven-year-old, I was annoyed that these boys, who had the same abilities, weren't expected to do housework. I was told off for being selfish when I said,

"No, I won't wash these dishes unless they do it too."

SAYING 'yes' TO SAYING 'NO'

I'll never forget what it felt like to be given the cold shoulder from the boys for the rest of the evening and, most of all, to disappoint my Gran.

Although I'd always been taught to say 'no' when faced with unfairness, I learned that people don't always practise what they preach.

From then on, I felt pressure to be a people pleaser. These messages were supported by demands from parents, teachers, friends and what I observed about the backlash that sometimes happens when girls and women say 'no' on TV.

There's an important difference between drawing a line in the sand in order to focus on your priorities, versus saying 'no' to be purposefully unhelpful, shirk on promises or wriggle out of taking responsibility. That's why it took years for me to realise that saying 'no' had nothing to do with me being mean or difficult, and everything to do with claiming my power.

ONCE I LEARNED TO UNDERSTAND THAT STATING 'NO' MEANS SAYING 'YES' TO MY DREAMS AND VALUES,

I BEGAN TO UNDERSTAND THAT 'NO' IS A POSITIVE TOOL.

You're invited to use 'no' as a complete sentence at least once this week, without apology. Your 'no' can take many forms, and the way you do it is up to you.

HERE'S A ROADMAP THAT MIGHT HELP YOU:

Say no to burning yourself out to get someone else's approval.

Say no to other people's judgements about who you are.

Say no to negative self-talk and forgive yourself.

Say no to a habit that is no longer serving you. For example, once my food allergies were identified, I stopped eating food that made me sick to be polite.

Say no to fear, and tell your fear who is in control: you.

Say no to something that feels like an obligation (unless it's homework or a promise you've already made) and choose inspiration instead.

Say no to _____.
(Choose your 'no'!)

The burden of other people's expectations can feel stifling. I know first-hand that this is easier said than done. We live in a culture that pressures us to have it all, be it all and do it all while supporting everyone but ourselves.

Let's embrace Chimamanda Ngozi Adichie's wisdom that,

"there are people who dislike you because you do not dislike yourself."

Recognise that setting healthier boundaries in our lives is a massive step towards caring for ourselves on a deeper level. It's worth the price of a few naysayers who may not have learned these lessons themselves yet.

STAY INTACT:
HOLD ON TO YOUR WHOLENESS. YOU ARE ENOUGH.

"DO YOUR HOMEWORK." "TRY HARDER." "HAVE YOU DONE YOUR CHORES?" "SECOND PLACE? NEXT TIME LET'S GO FOR FIRST."

Sound familiar? Growing up, I spent a lot of time focusing on being liked and seen as a 'good girl'. From Sunday school to the classroom, I absorbed the message that my worth was related to what I could do for others and how hard I worked. It took ages for me to realise that although being of service is meaningful, it is being – not doing – that defines human dignity.

No matter where we are on our path or how many times we stumble, we are enough. In a society that sometimes tells us we are broken for being less-than-perfect, it can be easy to forget that we are, by our very nature, intact.

I was reminded of this when I saw my favourite soul singer, the late Nina Simone, perform at a grand concert hall in Washington, DC. As Nina sang, "When you feel really low, there's a great truth you should know / When you're young, gifted and black, your soul's intact," the diverse crowd rose to its feet and echoed her words:

NINA SIMONE

"your soul's intact, that's a fact."

She permitted us to see ourselves as whole, to claim our value, and to remain rooted in who we are during change or hardship.

THROUGH NINA'S MUSICAL SCHOOLING, I LEARNED OUR PURPOSE IS TO BE TRUE TO OURSELVES.

Recognising the marvellous yet straightforward power of our existence helps us access a sense of peace and internal knowing. That's why I try to close my eyes, sit quietly and breathe into my questions or worries. It reminds me that being here is strength in itself when times are tough. Breath shows us that the most critical part of us is working, and the rest can always be figured out.

25

STEP INTO YOUR POWER

Pick your favourite quiet place and sit in a comfortable position. Place your hand over your heart, close your eyes and breathe. Next, visualise your future self. Imagine being so confident in who you are that no one else's views about you or ideas about your role are a factor. Pay attention to your mind and body.

Is it easy to see yourself and your worth without considering negative or positive input from others? Or, is it hard to think about who you are without hearing other people's voices of praise or critique? What does it feel like to be free of other people's expectations? What sensations are stirred up or disappear when you imagine your intact self on your terms?

Next, draw an image of yourself based on what you pictured during your meditation.

KEEP CALM

YOU BELONG! TAKE YOUR RIGHTFUL PLACE

What does 'belonging' mean to you? For me, it's about having a strong sense of self so that no matter what place you are in, you are rooted in your birthright, purpose. We all deserve to be secure in our identity.

Even though we live in a comparison-driven culture, we're all bonded by our common humanity. Although we may receive messages to the contrary, or have more or less access to status, no one of us is more valuable than the other.

To be sure, it is easier said than done to feel like we belong when we're in an environment with people who we share few things in common with, or when we're left out of group activities because we're new or different. That's why we must practise checking

in with ourselves and understanding the strengths we carry with us. This way, when something happens that moves us away from feeling comfortable in our own skin, we will be our own North Star, and bring ourselves back to the heart of our being.

We humans develop a lot of our ideas about who we are and where we fit in from our friends, family and the people we spend time with the most. We often share similar beliefs to the people nearest to us, which can have a positive influence, but sometimes makes us more close-minded or restless about trying new things and meeting new people.

While being a part of a group can help us discover who we are and teach us how to collaborate, we can be negatively impacted in spaces where we are isolated, pressured by our peers or expected to conform to unrealistic standards.

Since our social groups play a big role in impacting how we perceive ourselves in positive and negative ways, it is vital for us to be clear about which habits and beliefs are our own, and what we've adapted to fit in.

When I need help showing up in my fullest truth and realness, I think of my singer-songwriter friend, Morley's song, *Be the One*. She sings,

"IT'S ALRIGHT, TAKE YOUR RIGHTFUL PLACE... FEEL YOUR POWER IN THE WAY YOU DO WHAT YOU DO. BE THE ONE TO FIND A WAY OUT OF NO WAY. BE THE ONE TO OPEN DOORS AND STAND HEAD HELD HIGH,

STAND IN POINTED PLACES, AND MAKE THEM ROUND."

Her words always remind me to respect the groups I'm in, and to respect my truth by being sincerely myself. When I need to be reminded of the power I possess, I hum her tune about how finding belonging within helps us make a difference.

WHAT WORDS OR PICTURES REMIND YOU OF YOUR POWER AND BRING YOU BACK TO CENTRE?

→ STEP INTO YOUR POWER

If you don't have a motto yet or an image that brings you back to your core self, take some time to explore possibilities. Think about keeping these words and pictures close to you so they are always there when you need them.

When I need a pick-me-up or am feeling insecure in a new social setting, I often refer to a small wallet card I made that is etched with Maya Angelou's words:

> **"You alone are enough. You have nothing to prove to anybody."**

NiNA SIMONe

DeFINe YOURSELF:
Write your own life rules

"Follow the rules."

Chances are, you've heard these words countless times. In school and at home, rules can provide us with instructions that help keep us safe, organised, principled and on the same page with people in our community. Additionally, rules can also

Pelé

inform how we participate
and measure our progress in
sports, maths, school elections
and everything in between.

Although rules can benefit
us and teach us valuable
and necessary lessons, they
are also capable of being
flawed, biased, one-sided
or outdated. Whether they
are spoken or unspoken,
rules can become habits
and practices born from
expectations that no longer
fit the needs, diversity and
realities of our current society.

Pushing the limits of
traditional boundaries can
inspire creativity, expand
imaginations, offer fresh
perspectives or influence new
standards within an industry
– like the famous Brazilian
footballer, Pelé, known for his
unique 'ginga' footwork, or
the one-of-a-kind style of the
classically-trained pianist, jazz
singer and songwriter, Nina
Simone. From Dr. Martin
Luther King, Jr. to surrealist
Mexican artist Frida Kahlo,
trailblazing advocates and
artists throughout history

have shown us that there are times when not following 'the rules', or colouring outside the lines can help change the world. Although King and Kahlo are well-known examples of this, many other dreamers and everyday heroes display the faith, leadership and courage it takes to ask themselves and others who made the rules we're supposed to follow, how those rules could be improved to represent the wide-ranging diversity of humanity, and what they could do to offer new, more just and visionary ways of being and doing.

IN THAT SPIRIT, I CHALLENGE YOU TO THINK ABOUT THE RULES THAT GUIDE YOUR LIFE AND ASK YOURSELF WHICH ONES ALIGN WITH YOUR VISION AND PURPOSE, AND WHICH ONES DON'T. WHAT OLD RULES NEED TO BE LEFT BEHIND, AND WHICH NEW NORMS NEED TO EMERGE FOR THE TRUEST YOU TO SHINE THROUGH?

DR. MARTIN LUTHER KING, JR.

Frida Kahlo

STEP INTO YOUR POWER

On my sixteenth birthday, my family gave me a framed plaque of Colin Powell's short-but-sharp 'Rules of Leadership'. (Colin Powell was the first African-American to be appointed as US Secretary of State.) Although my family supported a different political party, they respected and valued his wisdom.

When I met Mr. Powell years later, I had an opportunity to share how much his rules have taught me (especially his sage words: "It Can Be Done.") As I rushed to express my gratitude quickly, while snapping a selfie of our time together, I thanked him for

motivating me to create my own life rules.

Based on his example, I made my own list that is always expanding as I learn from life's highs and lows. The rule on the top of my list is:

"Define yourself. Or, somebody else will."

What rules need to be created or rewritten in your life? Take my advice and define your own rules at the scale (ongoing, short-term, long-term) that works for you.

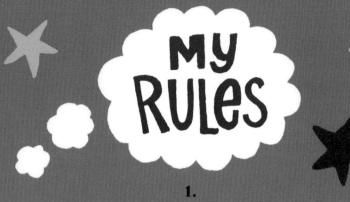

MY RULES

1.

First, sit down in a quiet place or a space with calming music. Then, close your eyes, put your hand on your heart, and listen to the whispers of your soul. You may call this reflection, meditation or whatever feels right for you. Listen to what comes up for you and honour it without judgement.

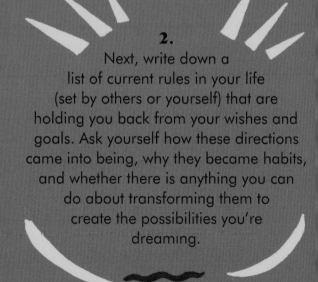

2.

Next, write down a list of current rules in your life (set by others or yourself) that are holding you back from your wishes and goals. Ask yourself how these directions came into being, why they became habits, and whether there is anything you can do about transforming them to create the possibilities you're dreaming.

3.

Then, write a journal entry that includes the origin story of the rules that don't work for you, and explore whether they are yours to own, or if they were passed down by others but might not fit into the plans you have for your life going forwards.

Journal

4.

When you're done, think about what you might do to help you sharpen your connection to what really stirs your heart and mind. For example, you may be part of a family where you feel pressured to try out for sports teams because everyone is an athlete, but you really want to focus on developing your artistic talent. Identify which rules in your life are ones you have adopted because of other people's expectations and which ones feel like they belong to you, your values and your passions.

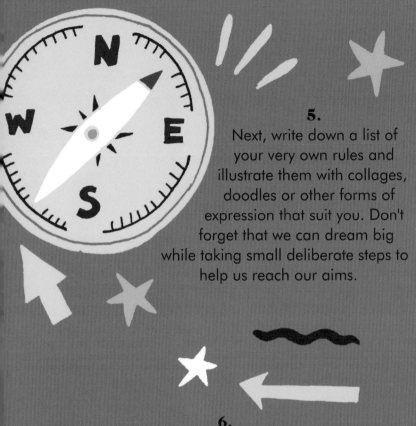

5.
Next, write down a list of
your very own rules and
illustrate them with collages,
doodles or other forms of
expression that suit you. Don't
forget that we can dream big
while taking small deliberate steps to
help us reach our aims.

6.
If some of the 'outside' rules you're dealing with are
fixed and beyond your control, think about what
choices you have the power to make. This allows
you to set intentions that help you feel closer to
navigating life with your own compass every day.

7.

Finally, draw a personal coat of arms. Don't worry about being fancy or official. Choose the colours, shapes, values, natural elements and motto that define you on your own terms. Once it is done, every time you're pushed to follow the crowd in the battle to be yourself, envision this crest as an imaginary shield you can wield with your spirit, actions, presence and voice. My personal crest depicts two dreadlocked mermaid lionesses with a chevron, which is a symbol for protection.

IT READS: FAITH. WISDOM. COURAGE. LOVE.

Community

LIFT AS YOU CLIMB:
Support your squad

FIND A MENTOR:
Learn from your heroes

ASK FOR HELP (Especially
when you need it most)

LIVE AND LET GO:
Dealing with drama, bullies
and fickle 'friends'

LIFT AS YOU
CLIMB
support your squad

Has a story ever etched itself onto your heart like the names of two friends carved onto a tree? When I was ten, *Hope for the Flowers*, an illustrated book about caterpillars moving through life's changes and growing as a result of collaboration became my holy text. A school librarian recommended Trina Paulus' brightly coloured book to me when I asked for a book that explores the meaning of life.

If you haven't read it yet, it's about Stripe and Yellow, two caterpillars seeking out their life path by trying to move up to the top of an endless tower of other climbing caterpillars. Along the way, they discover that stepping on other caterpillars and climbing to the top is not the key to transformation, and they choose to collaborate, take the risk of spinning cocoons and to emerge as butterflies, together.

Growing up, I thought of this book often when faced with social pressure to compete against other girlfriends instead of supporting them. A few years later, I remembered it when the most popular boy at school told me that I would be banished from sitting at the much-desired lunch bench we called 'the table' if I didn't stop talking to people he thought weren't cool enough for our crew.

Instead of playing into his game, I decided to invite several of the girls he wanted us to shun to join us. When the boy who I'll call 'Jack' gave me a nasty look and hissed that he was warning me, I said he could keep the table and that I'd be taking my new friends and all of the cupcakes I'd baked for everyone over to a bench. As I was walking away, one of the girls asked me if I was sure that I wanted to risk losing my place at 'the table'.

IT WAS THEN
THAT I KNEW
THAT I WAS
MOVING
INTO MY OWN
TRANSFORMATION,
AND THAT I
WAS TAKING A
LESSON FROM
MY BELOVED
CATERPILLARS
BY CHOOSING TO
FLY TOGETHER
INSTEAD OF
DIVIDING AND
CLIMBING.

STEP INTO YOUR POWER

I'm proud to know Ann Friedman and Aminatou Sow, two pals and authors of the book *Big Friendship*, who have taught me a lot about how to support your squad.

They created the term and idea of 'shine theory' which they define as:

"I don't shine if you don't shine. "

In a society that often pushes girls to compete, diminish or undermine each other's talents, 'shine theory' urges us to expand through supporting one another. The way I understand this is that 'if I win, you win' and vice versa. There's enough room for all of us to rise to the top and we're even stronger together.

Reach out to a friend and ask her how you can support her with a dream she's been holding on to. Tell her one thing every day this week you have noticed about how she shines brightly. Finally, if there's someone you admire but have been shy about approaching, reach out to her this week with a compliment, a kind note or an offer to hang out.

47

FIND A MENTOR:
LEARN FROM YOUR HEROES

Three years ago, my partner Travis was driving through New York City, when he brought up an interesting conversation he once had with a great jazz musician:

> **"You can learn how to read music and play an instrument in school, but there's nothing as powerful as creative community and really listening to the masters of their craft."**

Those words made me think about the people who moved me to find my ideas and voice: quirks, occasional self-doubt, meandering expression and all...

In my life, I have learned from three women – Lauryn Hill, Nina Simone and Erykah Badu. I've learned from studying their approach to their trade, and the way that they embody their work.

Learning life lessons from your role models is about trying on some of their traits for yourself, like being brave, speaking up, leading a group activity or doing something different from the norm.

Once you identify the characteristics that inspire you, see which ones fit with your soul. This isn't about copying or comparing yourself to another human. It's about seeing someone reflect the power and abilities you already possess. As simple as it might sound, I've come to believe that there is a Lauryn Hill or Erykah Badu song that deals with most of my trials and worries. Sometimes, when I'm feeling stuck or beaten down, and can't find the answers within myself, I imagine how the women who inspire me would respond to the situation. Erykah would tell me to breathe, "pack light" and hold on to myself. Lauryn would tell me that "respect is just a minimum." Even though I'm not a singer, these songstresses have taught me that what I do in the world is just as much about how I be.

Their soulful courage and sense of unconditional self-love (in a culture that often fails to recognise women of colour's worth and power) moves me. Each of these women has earned mainstream success while staying true to their values.

Their openness about themselves showed me that they have also struggled. It struck me that no matter what imperfections they revealed, I regarded them as powerful, wise and beautiful – regardless of impossible standards of beauty, life difficulty and other challenges. They made me feel heard, recognised, seen and understood.

I used to beat myself up for falling back into unhelpful patterns or shrinking myself to make other people feel comfortable, while my heart screamed that I should be bold.

I REALISE NOW THAT ALL THE FALLING, CRAWLING AND GETTING BACK UP ARE PARTS OF MY STORY.

⬤ STEP INTO YOUR POWER

Think about who your life muses are. Depending on your dreams, these might be leaders in the arts, sports, politics, history, science, travel, entertainment, food, environmental or literary worlds. Think about what you want to learn from these masters of craft, even if you never get to meet them. While their writings, ideas, songs, art, poems or performances may be representations of themselves that inspire you, think about their

presence, expression and the way they move in the world. Learn from their lessons about embracing who you are and accepting or even celebrating your shortcomings.

I have a feeling that if you do this, someday you'll be someone else's inspiration.

ASK FOR HELP

ESPECIALLY WHEN YOU NEED IT MOST

> "Help me if you can, I'm feeling down, and I do appreciate you being 'round, help me get my feet back on the ground, won't you please, please help me?"
>
> – The Beatles

What comes to mind when you think about asking for help? In elementary school, my friend Sarah held weekly Beatles-inspired dance parties in her apartment. Without fail, we'd dash around the den singing at the top of our lungs.

Today, I remember all of the lyrics to the songs we learned by heart. But, one tune surfaces when I'm overwhelmed, stressed, or hurting. The song 'Help!' became one of my anthems because its harmonious and relatable lyrics remind me of what it feels like to be supported and accepted. It taught me that asking for help (and giving it, too) is a normal and healthy part of life.

Some people will tell you that asking for help is a weakness. Some of my family and faculty

members at school certainly told me it was a flaw. But the Beatles' sunshiny song acknowledges that everyone needs help, and honours how common it is for people to need encouragement and companionship to feel more content, confident and secure.

If you're someone who struggles with asking for help, especially when you need it most, it's nothing to be ashamed of. We live in a culture where talking about finding and accessing support can be easier said than done. In a media climate that thrives on superhero stories about exceptional people, it's common to feel ashamed that our lives don't feel as effortless and straightforward as other people's might look on TV or in the glossy pages of your favourite magazine.

That's why it's vital for us to understand that offering help and receiving it are a key part of both strengthening relationships, and living well throughout our lives.

For those of us who find it easier to help others than to accept support from someone else, we must remember what they teach us every time we fly on a plane:

"PUT YOUR OXYGEN MASK ON FIRST, BEFORE HELPING OTHERS."

⊙ STEP INTO YOUR POWER

Whether you need a boost or ongoing support, you are not alone, even if it feels that way sometimes. From asking your parents or guidance counsellor for a tutor if you need to improve at school, to inquiring about summer classes to catch up after failing a course, there's no shame in taking action to get what you need to thrive. This also applies to your life outside of the classroom.

If you're troubled by bullying, fear, overwhelmedness, stress, sadness, worry, self-harm, extreme changes in your appetite or eating habits – or anything else – some people will have your back. While it can provide great comfort to confide in your friends, it's essential to seek advice from a trusted adult who can help you get what you need.

Nervous about asking the people closest to you for support? Consider reaching out to a counsellor at school or a therapist if you're having difficulties in your relationships with family, friends or other authority figures. If you have peer educators or coaches in your community, place of worship or school, connect with them to gather information, build bonds and learn about resources.

In most cases, it is good to partner with your parents or guardians on engaging a counsellor. If you don't feel safe doing this, ask your potential therapist these questions directly to help inform your decisions:

• Do you have experience working with people from my community/culture/background/religion/age?
• What are your legal obligations regarding parental involvement and consent?
• What are your confidentiality guidelines for minors?

Explore these questions and write down
your responses in your journal:

1. 'How does a (relationship/situation/
challenge/person) make me feel?'
2. 'What makes me feel supported?'
3. 'What would feeling better look and
feel like for me?'
4. 'What needs to change for that to happen
and what can I do to move it along?'

Practise sharing what you write down with
a parent or other dependable adult or a
trustworthy friend who may be
able to lend a hand.

RESOURCES OUTSIDE OF SCHOOL

- Need urgent support? If you're in the UK, text THEMIX to 85258 to speak to a trained texter who will listen and help you decide your next move. You can also call *Childline* for free on: 0800 1111 or the *Samaritans* on 116 123. For Australians, get in touch with *Lifeline* by texting 0477 13 11 14, and if you're a New Zealander, call 0800 54 37 54 to reach *Kidsline*'s 24-hour service.

- For questions and support about racial equality in the UK, find the *Equality and Human Rights Commission* online. You can also look up the *Runnymede Trust*: it is a thinktank that works to end racism. Visit *Voices that Shake!* online to get involved with forming a creative response to injustice, or book tickets to *Black Girl Fest*: a creative and cultural space to celebrate being a Black British girl. You can also visit *gal-dem* online or get a copy in print to read articles by young women of colour – and maybe even submit your own.

- Have questions about your body or relationships? Make an appointment with your GP or local Family Planning clinic. They often have clinics especially for young people.

- To access LGBTQ+ support in the UK, contact *Stonewall* online.

- For gender equality, health and the well-being of girls and women, visit *Women Deliver* online.

Don't forget, you can also set up your own organisation if you can't find one that exists. There will be plenty of people out there thinking the same things as you.

LIVE AND LET GO

Dealing with drama, bullies, and fickle friends

Do you believe in ghosts? I know I do, but not the kind that we dress up like for Halloween. I'm talking about fair-weather friends who only appear during times of good fortune and become hard to get hold of when you need help. Or, frenemies who look and act like friends one day, and then treat you terribly.

My first memory of a soured friendship goes back to first grade. Although I was one of a few black students in a mostly white class, I never felt left out until the day one of my classmates invited the entire class to her birthday party, except for me. Since we played together every day, I figured she must have forgotten to add my name to the guest list. I imagined every other response than the mocking words that spewed out of her mouth in front of a crowd, "Mum doesn't like blacks because she says you guys are bad. I don't want to be your friend anymore." My encounter with discrimination and betrayal left an imprint on my heart. For years, I thought of how sick it made me feel every time someone picked on me. I needed to be a friend to myself by facing my feelings, releasing shame and taking steps to build connections with people who share my values.

Discovering how to let go of relationships that hurt more than they help is challenging. It takes time to realise that our personal feelings, actions and responses are ours to own, and we're not responsible for other people's inability to return generosity or love.

RELATIONSHIPS MAY SHIFT BUT WILL ALWAYS RESULT IN A LESSON.

Whenever I would introduce a new friend to my mother, she'd say, "Friends come into your life for a reason, for a season or for a lifetime, which one do you think this one is?" It was her reminder to focus on how I want to show up in the world versus the outcome I want from others. Although we can't control people's behaviour, we can focus our energy on setting boundaries and modelling the deeds we want to see in the world. Since experts agree that friendships with people who celebrate our goals and support us boost our wellbeing, it's important to invest in them.

CONNECTIONS WITH FRIENDS WE CAN GROW WITH DIMINISH OUR STRESS, GIVE US A SENSE OF BELONGING, AND STRENGTHEN OUR SELF-CONFIDENCE.

➡ STEP INTO YOUR POWER

Take stock of the people you interact with the most on a daily basis.

Ask yourself the following questions:

1. Is my energy level high when this person is around?

2. Are they usually supportive?

3. Do they give as much as they take?

4. Do they apologise when they have made a mistake? Do they support me when I have made mistakes?

5. Is my energy level low when this person is around?

6. Do they often belittle, criticise, name-call or judge me? Do I associate this person with the negative voice in my head?

7. Do they make me feel like I have to be someone other than myself to be their friend?

8. Do they try to pressure me to do things I don't want to do?

If you answered yes to 1–4, consider writing notes of appreciation to the people in your life who support you, and write down qualities they possess that inspire you and how you approach friendship.

If you answered yes to 5–8, these relationships are either unhealthy, draining or need improvement. Think about whether you feel comfortable talking with them about what needs to change or whether you'd feel happier if you moved on. If so, it's time to refocus your energy on your passions and bonding with folks who uplift you.

If you are experiencing stress, anxiety or abuse, keep a trusted adult informed and talk to a counsellor about coping tools and ways to heal.

CHOICES

TAKE HEART AND TRUST YOUR GUT

ASK FOR IT:
Own what you want

DON'T FIT IN?
Pave new ground

BE YOU, NOT 'PERFECT'

TAKE HEART

TRUST YOUR GUT

Do you ever struggle with making decisions? The good news is that we come equipped with a compass that tells us what to do: our gut. Like all animals, we humans use our instincts to cope with changes, determine direction, protect ourselves and survive. Our internal sat-nav is a tool that our ancestors have relied on for centuries. While reason and critical thinking are important and should inform our actions, we're often taught to ignore the power of our intuition, which is often commonly referred to as **'trusting your gut' and 'following your heart'.**

While gut feelings aren't fail-safe and can be confused by bias, genuine mistakes and hasty judgements, they can help us deepen our awareness about our surroundings, improve with time and experience and provide valuable knowledge through lessons learned in the past. Although our guts can't speak to us in English, they communicate in another native tongue: through nerve signals to our brains and our tummies.

Our instinct is our inner voice and it is important to pay attention whether it whispers or it roars. As someone who considers herself a highly sensitive person, I always bristled at the limitations of the quip "feelings are not facts." Although I love logical evidence, we often just 'know' when things are wrong because our bodies tell us so.

Have you ever seen someone trying to copy off of your paper in school and it made your stomach hurt? Or have you ever felt uncomfortable because you have been asked to keep a secret that you know could get you or someone else in trouble? Do you ever feel like you don't want to hug a stranger even if you're being encouraged to do so? The icky 'uh-oh' reactions you might feel in your body and mind are signals that something is off.

OUR BODIES POSSESS A WISDOM THAT CAN HELP GUIDE US, HEAL US AND PROTECT OURSELVES. TUNE IN AND LISTEN.

STEP INTO YOUR POWER

No matter whether your situation is related to safety, or if you're mulling over a decision, it's important to listen to your intuition because it serves us best when we give it plenty of practice.

HERE ARE A FEW PRO-TIPS...

- Write a list of three times you listened to your gut or followed your heart

- Next, write three times you wished that you followed your intuition but didn't. Jot down what you learned.

- Outline your body on a piece of paper. Label what feelings you experience and where when you're excited, fearful, anxious, nervous, overwhelmed, tense, comfortable or content.

69

ASK FOR IT:
OWN WHAT YOU WANT

I was born a diplomat. Or, at least this is what my parents said when they joked about my natural negotiation skills.

Years before I even understood what the word 'negotiation' meant, I was clear about what I wanted, who might help me achieve it and, often, how it might result in helpful outcomes for others.

Whether I was appealing to my parents about extending my bedtime so I could read my favourite books for longer, or bartering with shopkeepers over whether they could lower their 'best price' at my local market, I discovered that I felt most powerful when I embraced my urge to ask for more. Once, I owned my power by questioning a teacher who graded me less than male schoolmates on a group project where I did most of the work. I challenged him and said I wanted our grades to reflect our efforts equally – and after some initial discomfort and a frank conversation about my contributions to the project, it worked.

Although it was awkward to confront an adult about something thorny, my respectful but direct approach resulted in a positive change. Also, it opened his eyes to the fact that he was focusing attention on who had the loudest voices during our presentation, without regard for who put in hard work behind the scenes.

What I learned from these experiences is that a world of possibility exists between a firm 'yes' or 'no'. Unless we speak up and ask, we may never know if we could have had more options. To be sure, it is wise to use our best judgement when choosing when to push these limits, and it's most important to respect rules that prevent people from getting harmed or left out.

With that said, despite receiving mixed messages from adults about directly communicating my wants and needs, I understood deep down that I felt most powerful when I honestly expressed what I needed.

Even if it doesn't always turn out the way I hope, I have never regretted living by this motto, *Qui audet adipiscitur*, which translated from Latin means **'she who dares, wins'.**

Sam ___ A

Jamia ___ C+

Mike — — A-

GRADE BOOK

71

STEP INTO YOUR POWER

HAVE YOU EVER HELD YOURSELF BACK FROM ASKING FOR WHAT YOU WANT?

If yes, is it because you're afraid of being labelled 'bossy' or being excluded? I can guarantee from my experience that staying in the shadows or keeping silent won't help you get closer to your dreams.

TAKE THESE STEPS:

1. Get to know yourself. Is there something about your own self-talk that is making you doubt your worth? If so, work on building up your confidence.

2. Ask for what you want every day this week, and do so without apologising, looking down or avoiding eye contact.

3. Let go. If you meet criticism, awkwardness, or the silent treatment as a response, it doesn't mean your request or you are the problem. In fact, it could be someone else getting used to a shift in the power dynamic or merely being unable to meet your need. Don't take it personally, accept my congrats for being true to yourself, and take the lesson with you.

DON'T FIT IN?

When I was 18, I enrolled at university to study my passion, broadcast journalism. Whenever CNN flashed on the screen, I pictured my future self: an award-winning global journalist and fearless front-line correspondent like my childhood idol Christiane Amanpour – except with long kinky braids and brown skin.

Then, something shocking happened. My teacher, an older white male professor, peered down at me through his glasses and said, "I'd hate to see you waste your articulateness. You are well-spoken, have a young face and you'll enjoy a long shelf-life in the media field, but you'll have to straighten your hair in order to be taken seriously in media." As if that wasn't bad enough, he went on to challenge me to identify "one black woman with [natural] hair like yours on a major media network" to prove his point.

My stomach churned when I heard someone I looked up to tell me that I would need to change myself, my appearance and the hair type I was born with to be on camera. I knew that my ideas and my mind were more important than the texture of my curls. Still, it hurt to be told that my voice would not matter unless it was packaged in a body that fit a very narrow beauty standard.

Years later, when I was asked to represent my job on a major TV network, I thanked this professor for driving me towards my media activism, publishing and public speaking work.

Pave New Ground

Although our interaction was initially painful and unjust, it taught me a valuable lesson. Now, instead of asking myself what I need to do to be included, I wonder what I can build to pave new ground without shrinking myself. My professor also taught me that just because someone else might underestimate you it doesn't mean they are right.

IF THEY MISUNDERSTAND YOUR POWER, IT'S THEIR LOSS, BECAUSE AS LONG AS YOU KNOW THAT YOU CAN DO ANYTHING YOU SET YOUR MIND TO, YOU'RE ON THE ROAD TO VICTORY.

➡ STEP INTO YOUR POWER

My friend Carolyn often says, **"Don't give away your power,"** when she sees me or others listening to naysayers instead of owning our own abilities, skills, talents and value.

Make a pledge to yourself to write down what power you do have and what you can build or create with it next time you find yourself in a situation where someone or something makes you feel like you don't belong.

Next, take what you write and turn it into an action plan. Jot down the following prompt.

This month I will take these three steps towards chasing my dream. Maybe you're good at art. Make it happen by committing to draw for at least 15 minutes a day; drawing your own version of a Google doodle and applying for their annual contest; and starting your own Instagram feed featuring your original designs. (Check with an adult first before joining social media sites.)

Be you, Not "perfect"

Throughout my life, I have seen how the media impacts how we see ourselves, our voices and our bodies. I remember growing up and having my parents sit me down at dinner to 'de-program' me when I wanted to straighten my hair so I could have a silky side-pony tail like girls I saw on TV instead of an afro-puff, or wondering why in Saudi Arabia where

I grew up as an ex-pat, some of my schoolmates focused on looking like US and European TV stars, bleaching their skin and hair, and shrinking themselves in order to fit a narrow vision of beauty. It seemed to me that the pressure to fit into 'the mould' drained so much energy that could have been channelled into joy.

It was disturbing to see so much focus being put on girls' looks instead of our views, from the movie theatre to magazines and even in school and athletics. Author and activist Gloria Steinem taught me that **"the trouble is that women in the media are treated like ornaments and not instruments."** I understood that there was nothing wrong with me, or us. Instead, the problem was with the system and culture that has been teaching girls and young women that we have to be perfect or contort ourselves into everyone else's vision of who we should be instead of ourselves.

Sadly, since you live in the same world I'm inhabiting, I'm sure you've encountered similar pressures to do everything right, excel while making it look effortless, look put-together all the time and do it all with a smile at some point in your life.

That's why I'm here to say, let's bid farewell to all of that. Perfection doesn't exist, and that's a good thing. We're not robots. We're living, breathing, thriving organisms that are always growing and evolving in all of our pain, beauty, curiosity, vulnerability and strength. You never need permission to be yourself. You don't need to look like anyone but yourself; you don't have to define yourself by other people's judgements; and your hunger does not need to be ignored.

THE
TRUTH IS,
EVERY ONE
OF US IS
PERFECTLY
IMPERFECT,

AND THAT'S WHAT MAKES US DIVERSE AND EXCITING.

◁ STEP INTO YOUR POWER

Tell a friend everything you love about who she is and how she shows up in the world.

Tell her about all of the things you appreciate about her and how her actions, ideas, unique quirks and skills impact your life.

HAVE FUN WITH IT!

Later, write in your journal about what it felt like to share your observations about this person. Imagine what it would feel like to talk to yourself in the same way when you're feeling pressure to be anyone but your stunning, singular one-of-a-kind self.

SPEAK TRUTH TO ADULTS:
Know your rights and take action

DON'T AGONISE, ORGANISE:
Create what you need

IN A RUT? GET UNSTUCK!

BRANCH OUT:
Find your crew

SPEAK TRUTH TO ADULTS

KNOW YOUR RIGHTS & TAKE ACTION

Do you ever feel like adults tell you what to believe more often than they ask for your opinion? Studies show that our thoughts about policies, governments and power are influenced by our closest relatives. That's why it's important to educate yourself about your rights, stay up to date on current events and determine what inspires you.

Although we don't always hold the same viewpoints as our family, our upbringing may shape our political ideas over

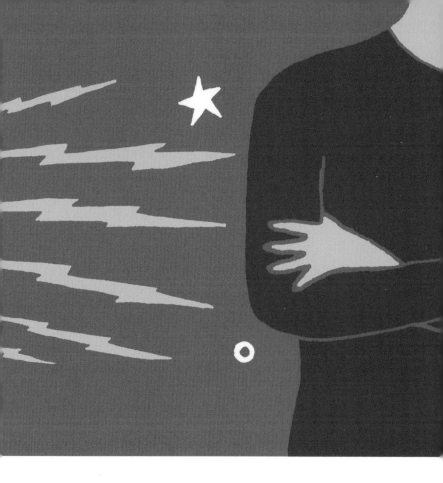

time. If your parents push you to adopt their perspective, they may influence your beliefs in the future. Even if you rebel as a kid or teenager, in adulthood, people generally return to the political leanings they were raised with.

People often argue without remembering that most of us want similar goals – **freedom, justice, safety and personal choice.** The tricky part is that people often hold different visions about how to achieve those goals.

It's okay to disagree with the people we care about and to trust our own feelings as our ideas evolve. We're all impacted by the culture and systems we live with, but the solutions we envision for the world's problems may be different from our parents or friends.

For some, the existing structure comes with benefits, and for others, setbacks. That's why it's important to learn as much as you can about the laws, policies and cultural norms that impact your community and beyond. Once you know what matters most to you, you can take part in changing what needs to be fixed.

If you're prepared with basic information about how your school, community or government works, you're in a better position to achieve the progress you're seeking.

It's always a good time to understand how to support yourself and your values.

YOU DON'T HAVE TO WAIT UNTIL YOU'VE BEEN MISTREATED, WITNESSED INJUSTICE OR WANT TO CHANGE A RULE TO EDUCATE YOURSELF AND MAKE YOUR VOICE HEARD.

STEP INTO YOUR POWER

HERE ARE SOME WAYS YOU CAN TAKE ACTION:

Congratulations! You have been elected leader of your country for the duration of this exercise. Write or record the speech you would give to your citizens.

Read the **UN Convention on the Rights of the Child** to understand your rights as a young person. Consider joining Model United Nations or your school debate club.

Regularly read your local newspaper, and one from abroad, to understand timely topics from diverse perspectives. You can also do this via news sites, streaming, podcast and radio news shows.

Explore your legal rights and your local constitution via a civics class, and through online research.

Practise speaking up in the ways that feel right for you. This could be via blogs or vlogs, creating or signing petitions, or making zines, documentaries or posters.

SPEAK OUT
create a CAMPAIGN
VOLUNTEER
Get involved
SERVE
SAY IT LOUD
TALK

DON'T AGONISE, ORGANISE
create what you need

Do you ever feel like the weight of the world's injustices is so heavy that it's hard to figure out how to take action? Don't worry, it's normal to feel overwhelmed by a chaotic political landscape and a media cycle that never sleeps.

Although it can be tempting to curl up and hide when we see a problem that needs fixing, we always have the power to choose to take a stand. I learned this from my parents who grew up in the segregated Southern US during the 1960s.

My mother's memories about her involvement with rallies and teach-ins during high school and, most of all, her story about marching on Washington with Dr. Martin Luther King inspired me. I asked her repeatedly to tell me about what she felt while she sat-in at segregated lunch counters, or registered voters in spite of pressure and unfair punishment.

Years later, my activism was born on the playground when I told off bullies for taunting other kids. I participated in my first anti-racist protest at the age of 10 with my parents. Some of my classmates had nicknamed me 'Rebel with a Cause', and I lived up to it. I set up recycling campaigns at school, ran for class president and passed petitions to fight apartheid in South Africa.

When I studied the women's rights movement in the sixties a few years later, I learned about the late black feminist firebrand Florynce 'Flo' Kennedy, who said, "The biggest sin is sitting on your [bum]... Don't agonise. Organise." Her legacy and call to action continues to resonate with the rising tide of resistance worldwide.

We all benefit from supporting each other's right and access to free speech, assembly and media that help us make informed decisions about our lives.

While it can be intimidating when we're not able to find the 'right' words, or the absolute best approach to making a difference, being a part of the solution is more important than perfection. Why? Because if not us, me and you, then who?

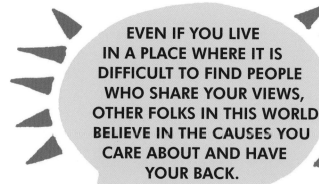

EVEN IF YOU LIVE IN A PLACE WHERE IT IS DIFFICULT TO FIND PEOPLE WHO SHARE YOUR VIEWS, OTHER FOLKS IN THIS WORLD BELIEVE IN THE CAUSES YOU CARE ABOUT AND HAVE YOUR BACK.

STEP INTO YOUR POWER

POPULAR CULTURE MOVES HEARTS AND MINDS AND PLAYS A MAJOR ROLE IN SHAPING OUR ATTITUDES.

Choose a past or present movement that interests you and discover as much as you can about it through reading activist biographies and memoirs, and watching documentary films online or in the library. Next, create and share a political poster, zine or political newsletter, infographic, meme, podcast or vlog about what you've learned.

Integrate your interest in activism into your schoolwork. Do a presentation about what you've learned and how you can apply it to a current or local issue you would like to take on. Consider joining an existing group or club focused on activism at your school, community centre, or house of worship. Or, start a new campaign with your friends or other like-minded people.

IN A RUT?

Get unstuck!

Have you ever felt like you're living in a real-life quicksand scene from a cartoon? Or do you ever feel like you're running on a treadmill with no end in sight? If so, you're like me, and many other humans who have at some point in our lives felt stuck.

Sometimes we're up against the wall of ourselves, and it's hard to imagine a better future than what's in front of us. Whether you're clinging to a bad habit, feeling under-motivated or keep criticising yourself after making a mistake, it can be hard to rise out of, around, under or above a stubborn rock of a rut.

In some cases, there are real challenges in our way that prevent us from moving forwards. We're often held back by our fear of losing control, a lack of confidence or feeling overwhelmed by pressure or judgement from the people around us. Mostly, our doubts about the real power we do have in the face of difficulty contribute to us getting in our own way. Since it took me many years to learn to spot how I might be playing a role in holding myself back (even in the face of solid challenges) I thought I'd save you some time and hopefully some hard-fought lessons.

Although this book is too short for me to list all of the times I've had to crawl, push, dance and march my way out of mental potholes that prevented me from understanding how to own and harvest my abilities and insights, I thought I'd share the two questions I ask myself when times get tough.

AND "WHAT CHOICE DO I HAVE THE POWER TO MAKE?"

⊃ STEP INTO YOUR POWER

IN A SLUMP?

First, know your value. You matter, full stop – not because of what you do, but because of who you are.

Then, see it for what it is and say out loud,

"I see you for who you are. I accept you, and like everything else, this too shall pass. I choose to let you go and claim my power."

I know this might sound silly, but ruts are bullies, and we never back down from those.

Next, make a list of baby-steps you can take to get closer to your goal and write them down or type them into your planner.

Finally, move your body and shift your mind. When I'm feeling stuck, I jump on my trampoline, do mood-boosting method workouts that combine dance, positive affirmations and martial arts, hold a dance party of one in my living room to shake off stuck energy, or take a walk in the park before returning to my writing, cleaning, drawing, French class homework or other projects I've put off.

BRANCH OUT: FIND YOUR CREW

Do you ever wish you had more people in your life who understand and support you? Despite all of the buddy flicks and squad shows on TV, finding friends we can rely on can be easier said than done. Whether you have a ton of friends you've known from the start, or you're feeling lonely because you've started attending a new school, it can be tough to open up and build new relationships. But, stepping out of your comfort zone to meet folks who fascinate and encourage you can broaden your outlook and enrich your life.

If you're interested in making new connections or need a support network with hobbies and goals that match yours, reach out. Opening up and interacting with people outside of your inner circle can be scary but it almost always delivers positive results.

Working with Andrea Pippins on *Young, Gifted and Black* and now, *Step into My Power* has affirmed my belief in branching out. If we hadn't reached out to each other many years ago, we would have missed out on a beautiful partnership that is still growing.

JAMIA WILSON

ANDREA PIPPINS

BY LETTING GO OF CLOSED-OFF CLIQUES AND MAKING YOUR FRIEND GROUP INCLUSIVE, YOU EXPAND YOUR EXPOSURE TO NEW SKILLS, CULTURES AND IDEAS. IT'S A GREAT WAY TO EXPERIENCE ACCEPTANCE, BELONGING AND RECIPROCITY, AND IN TURN, OFFER THAT FEELING TO OTHERS.

STEP INTO YOUR POWER

DO YOU HAVE TROUBLE INTRODUCING YOURSELF?

Here are a few short phrases you can practise while making eye contact, standing or sitting up, extending a smile and offering a handshake – if it feels appropriate. People love compliments, so don't be afraid to share if you've heard about their talent or unique skills or interests too!

• "Hi, my name is _____, I'm in_____ school / class and I'm really interested in learning about the _____club you organised. It's nice to meet you. How are you?"

• If you've heard about them through a mutual friend, or you have other common ground or connections, mention it to break the ice. "I've heard wonderful things about you and your singing from our mutual friend Rachel! My name is _____. Nice to meet you!"

• After you introduce yourself, start out by asking your new friend questions about their passions. Listen deeply, make eye contact and avoid distractions like looking at your phone. You're paving the way to discover common ground.

• Be aware of body language and non-verbal cues. Humans do a lot of our communicating through our bodies. If you notice that someone is keeping a bit of distance or not comfortable with hugging or touching, respect their boundaries and don't take it personally.

• Practise telling your personal story, so you're ready when you're engaging new people. I use leadership expert Marshall Ganz's 'story of self, story of us, story of now' framework to help me create a narrative of my life that reflects my values and passions. By telling your own story, it will also inspire your new pal to share their own.

1. The 'story of self' helps you introduce who you are as a person – an artist, an advocate, a student, a volunteer, an athlete, etc.

2. The 'story of us' gives you a chance to say how you or your passion relates to what you're trying to do in school or the community or the world.

3. And the 'story of now' is telling a new friend about why you're passionate about X or Y, and providing a takeaway about how they can get involved.

WHERE TO FIND YOUR GREAT NEW FRIEND:

• Join an organisation that empowers girls. Organisations like Girl Scouts and Girl Guides organise opportunities for young women to learn skills, participate in cultural and educational activities, collaborate and lead.

• Go to summer camp. Camp is a great place to find your squad (and make new pen pals if they live far away) because everyone shares a common experience of being in a new environment and trying new adventures.

• Follow your interests. Go to a music centre or sports club to find people with shared interests.

• If funding is a concern, some sleep-away and day camps offer scholarship programmes to help with the cost, and others are sponsored by charities who offer tuition for free. Ask your school or teacher for more information.

• Follow up. If you've met someone new on a field trip or outing with your school, be sure to reach out afterwards to let them know you enjoyed meeting them. Make sure to mention something you remembered about your time together or a common experience you shared, and invite them to stay in touch.

SELF-CARE

BE KIND TO YOURSELF

LISTEN TO YOUR BODY

DEALING WITH ILLNESS

FIND THE LESSON:
Bounce back from the dumps,
failures and other bummers

**SHINE BRIGHTLY WITHOUT
BURNING OUT**

Be Kind to YOURSElf

For me, few words have left my heart throbbing more than something my friend Kathleen said one day when I was speaking about a tough time I was going through.

At the end of my rant about the volcano of stress I was feeling, she said, "Wow. The way you talk to yourself is far too harsh. You're kind to everyone but yourself. Give yourself a break. It doesn't have to be this hard. Breathe." Does this sound familiar?

At the time, I was startled by the force of the truth she shared. But I listened to her advice and took a deep breath… I was embarrassed that my friend had seen me so clearly, and angry about feeling exposed. At the same time, I knew she was right. For as long as I can remember, I have wrestled with slaying the dragons of my expectations. I realised I had cared for others, but not for my own body and spirit. As someone who has lived with a disability my entire life, I spent so much time uncomfortably pushing myself to adapt so I could be "normal" that I lost sight of the fact that everyone is entitled to self-care – including me, and including you.

After my conversation with Kathleen, I attempted to write down my thoughts for a few hours. Now that we'd had this conversation, my mind was swirling with what I took as criticism, and I burned with shame, sadness and fear that something was wrong with me because I wasn't practising self-care as well as the people around me.

Sometimes our harshest critics are in our own heads.

I realised that this pattern of thought was a textbook example of what Kathleen described. At that moment, I acknowledged that her comment collided with my fears of being hurt or cast out. Fears that came from past experiences with bullying and encounters with discrimination. We all encounter self-doubt from time to time, but it was painful to hear someone else comment on my own struggle with negative thoughts.

Once I allowed myself some quiet and space, I realised where and when I had been taught to be unkind to myself. Only then was I able to face reality, and start taking steps to change my relationship to my most reliable and enduring friend – myself.

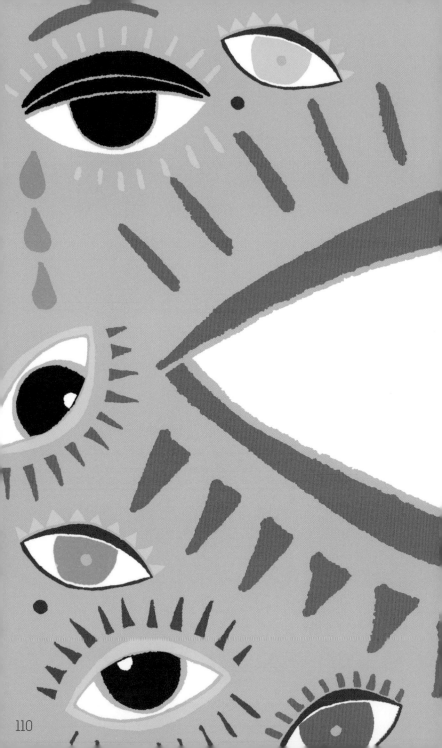

SOMETIMES THE
PEOPLE YOU LOVE
SEEM TO SEE YOU
MORE CLEARLY THAN
YOU DO YOURSELF.
THIS ALSO MEANS
THEY CAN SAY THINGS
THAT CUT TO
YOUR CORE.

STEP INTO YOUR POWER

If you're stubborn like me, you might need to hear why being kinder to yourself can make you more helpful to the people you adore. If you've been on a plane, you'll remember how the flight attendants instruct you to put your oxygen mask on first before helping others. I often think of this message when I'm feeling overwhelmed, notice pain in my body or anxiety in my mind.

Try writing in a **gratitude journal** every day. It can help you treat yourself the way you aspire to treat others: with kindness and love. Before I go to bed, I write down everything and everyone I'm grateful for.

When I wake up the next morning, I write down an affirmation for the day. One of my statements is: "I let go of yesterday; I embrace today I am enough, and I have what it takes." What's yours?

113

LISTEN TO YOUR BODY

Do you trust your body, your longest faithful friend? Our bodies heal, protect, and move us through our lives, but we don't always take time to check in and pay attention to what's happening inside of us.

It's important to tune into our body's messages to hear what it needs. We can then pinpoint and address challenges before they become a problem. In turn, we can also discover what feels good so that we can give our bodies more of what makes them flourish.

Whether it whispers hints through gut intuition, or roars in the form of discomfort or pain, our bodies are designed to work for and with us every day. Since we're often moving swiftly in a fast-paced world, we can forget everything our body does for us until something goes awry. My body always lets me know that she ultimately calls all the shots. As someone who has wrestled with long-standing health issues throughout my life, I've learned to listen to the hints my body offers and take them seriously. When something feels out of order, it's time to observe our body's signals so we can provide the food, sleep, rest, water, fresh air or other support It requires. Alternatively, when something like yoga soothes me into a place of peace, it's a reminder that my body responds positively to relaxation and stretching.

eat

drink water

ALTHOUGH WE ALL
HAVE DIFFERENT
BODY TYPES, SIZES,
COLOURS, AND
SHAPES WE ALL
BENEFIT FROM
UNDERSTANDING
OUR BODY'S
UNIQUE VOICE,
AND GIVING
IT THE MOVEMENT,
TRANQUILITY,
STRETCHING OR
SUPPORT IT NEEDS.

meditate

STEP INTO YOUR POWER

- **Check in with your body.**

Take time to concentrate on your body throughout the day. Notice what you're feeling in your gut, your joints and in your back. Do you feel clenched or at ease? Do you notice these symptoms arising in certain spaces or around specific people or situations? If so, talk to a trustworthy adult about connecting with a therapist.

- **Jumpstart each day.**

Need a little jolt to wake you up in the morning? Do ten jumping jacks or hop on a mini trampoline to kick-start your energy and release tension. I do this whenever I start a writing project and need a surge of creativity.

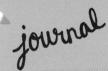

journal

exercise

- **Keep breathing.**

Next time you feel tense, uncomfortable, tired or jittery, take a deep inhale in through your nose. Next, push your right nostril and exhale out of the left side of your nose. Follow this by inhaling with the left nostril and then pushing on it while you exhale through the right nostril. Afterwards, swap nostrils and alternate between them. If you feel silly, do it in a private space. This breathing practice comes from yoga.

• Lay it out.

If you need to wind down after a busy day, lie down flat on your back in a quiet space. Close your eyes. Imagine yourself releasing anything that feels heavy, stressful or worrisome into the ground below you. Picture yourself sinking closer to the Earth, vertebra by vertebra, until you feel more peaceful. Envision all of the stress melting off of your body in the form of imaginary seeds that fall to the ground and will re-emerge as new energy in bloom.

• Catch your ZZZs.

If you're always tired or feeling exhausted throughout the day, try sleeping at the same time every night and waking up at the same time every day to train your body. If you have trouble resting through the night, ask a trusted adult to take you to the doctor for more support.

- **Talk about it.**

If you're feeling under the weather or experiencing symptoms of discomfort, soreness or pain, reach out to a dependable adult and a healthcare provider you trust for help. Put prevention first and get help sooner rather than later to ensure the best outcome.

- **Keep your energy up.**

Always eat breakfast to ensure that you can get-up-and-go without crashing later in the day. If you feel yourself moving slowly or feeling listless, feed yourself protein-rich snacks and water to stay nourished.

119

DeALING WITH ILLNeSS

Do you live with a chronic illness? I do. Over the years, I have slowly accepted the fact that my body is sensitive and requires extra attention to self-care. Instead of being distressed about the fact that it functions differently than others', I've shifted my focus towards how it has expanded my sense of what matters most in my life.

After years of apologising and feeling guilty for something that is out of my control, I have embraced that my body is my ultimate spiritual teacher. She's a perfectly flawed teacher who forces me to listen to the messages I'm getting from aches and pain, to drink water like a mermaid and to cherish sleep as if it were holy, because it's the minimum my body needs to prosper.

For me, acceptance is not giving up. I can't say that having an illness of any kind is easy or fun, but I can say that managing treatment in partnership with my doctors and caretakers, and developing coping strategies, gets better with time. While I'm not a doctor or nurse, I know how it feels to feel vulnerable and frustrated when your body won't cooperate with your plans.

Being tired or sick does not define you or anyone else, even if it sometimes feels that way. Illness is a part of the human experience and it is never your fault. If you've just been diagnosed, you might feel uncomfortable, scared or disappointed. It's perfectly normal to process feelings that arise or to want to have time to think about your situation before talking about it. It is hard to comprehend how difficult a health condition can be until you have one. But, I have a greater respect for what it takes for people to get out of bed, show up, follow through and create things when they are managing an illness. I also understand that above all else, taking the time and space you need to heal your body is more important than anything else.

THAT'S WHY I'M
SHARING WHAT I'VE
LEARNED TO HELP ME
OVERCOME FLARE-UPS,
OVERWHELMEDNESS,
SLUGGISHNESS,
STRESSFUL DOCTOR'S
VISITS AND MORE.

STEP INTO YOUR POWER

* Start a wellness journal.

Jot down a few sentences in the morning and evening about how you feel with different kinds of weather, sleep patterns, stress levels and different kinds of food and hydration. If you're experiencing pain, note what level of discomfort you feel when you wake up in the morning and when you go to bed at night. At the end of the week, note what was helpful and unhelpful.

* Trust yourself.

Doctors and other healers are important partners on the path to healing. But like any other humans, doctors aren't always perfect. You are the boss of your body. You know how your body feels more than anyone else does. If any doctor, nurse or other health professional tells you that your suffering is 'all in your head', talk with a trusted adult and seek a second, and third, professional opinion. Practise asking any questions you have before your appointment.

* Educate your loved ones.

Sometimes when we're feeling our worst, the people close to us don't know what to do. Take time to share with your family and best friends how they can help you. Don't be shy about asking a friend to bring you missed homework, or your parents to talk with your teachers if you need extra time, regular bathroom breaks or other health accommodations.

* Join the party wherever you are.

If you're not able to attend an event or access an activity, remind yourself that 'there's always more fun to be had' and ask your friends to Skype or FaceTime, so that you can participate in the action from afar. Catch the silver lining if you're upset about missing out. You now have time for napping, pyjama-wearing, video game-playing, TV marathons, pet-cuddling, and daydreaming while you recover.

* **Be present for others.** If it's your loved one who is sick, listen deeply, ask how you can help and simply say, "I'm here for you, what can I do to support you?" Some people may be too tired to think about what they need, so offer to help bring them meals, run errands, watch TV with them or simply to be a listening ear.

* **Be proactive.** Work with your teachers and guidance counsellor at school to create a plan for you to get notes, homework and updates when and if you have to miss school or arrive late because you're sick. If you know what triggers flare-ups, consider making plans that might help, like going to bed early, eating foods you digest well or taking a relaxing bath on the night before a big test, presentation or sporting event.

* **Be gentle with yourself.** Carry small versions of the creature comforts you need with you in case you are away from home when you're feeling ill.

* Kindly set boundaries without apology. If you have special requirements, it's no one's business but yours and the people entrusted with your care. You can choose to explain why you might need an allergy-free lunch, a wheelchair-accessible desk, audiobooks, or a voice-recorder for note-taking in class, but that's your decision. Practise saying: "I appreciate your interest, but it's a personal matter."

* Let it go. I'll never forget how mortified I was when I threw up in the classroom in front of my classmates. When I returned to school, I learned that most people were worried about me and simply wanted to know that I was okay. Be gentle with yourself, and remember that everyone gets sick or knows someone who has been sick. People will forget as soon as Beyoncé drops a new album or something else big happens.

* Have hope. Together with your trusted adults, you will find a routine of care that works for you. Find small things that help when you're feeling run down. Maybe that's a cup of tea, warm blankets or a hot-water bottle.

FIND THE LESSON:

bounce back from the dumps, failures, and other bummers

Do you ever struggle with catching the silver lining in the aftermath of a let-down? When hurt, hardship, and sorrow come my way, I imagine myself as a tree in a field over the course of four seasons.

As I envisage the elements that might impact the tree through sunny days, windy storms, winter chills and even broken branches, I hark back to the fact that a tree is still a tree in any kind of weather. When the fruits of the tree fall to the ground, I picture the seeds returning to the earth, and sprouting into blooms as a result of time and nourishment.

My go-to daydream reminds me of the first time I heard author and activist Glennon Melton Doyle's motto, **"First the pain, then the rising."** I met Glennon during a time when my broken heart needed mending and I received her words as a soothing-but-forceful call to action, and a reminder that we as humans are as resilient as my imaginary tree.

AT SOME POINT DURING OUR LIFETIME THE CLIMATE MAY BE HARSH DUE TO ELEMENTS WITHIN OR OUTSIDE OF OUR CONTROL. DESPITE THIS, WE HAVE THE ABILITY TO FACE OUR DIFFICULTIES HEAD-ON, TO NURTURE OURSELVES WHEN WE'RE HURTING, AND TO GAIN STRENGTH AND WISDOM TO HELP GET US THROUGH THE NEXT TIME CHANGING WINDS BLOW THE LEAVES OFF OUR STURDY BRANCHES.

◉ STEP INTO YOUR POWER

A helpful way to move past our challenges is to face them, live through them, and accept the lessons they offer as an opportunity to grow. It's okay to acknowledge our disappointment and grief. It's a necessary part of processing our experiences and helps set the stage for us to release, reflect and rebuild as we turn the page on our pain to start our next chapter.

To be clear, accepting that something is a drag and that it impacted us, doesn't mean that it defines us or limits us from new opportunities in the future. It simply means that we are owning our experiences and their effect on us, and making a decision to learn about who we are and who we want to be moving forwards.

Think about a major hurdle you have overcome. Write down three things you learned about yourself during your time of difficulty. How did you show up at home, at school and with the people you care about? Would you have done anything differently now with time and perspective? How did you feel in your body during this time? Is there anything you've learned that you will use to nurture yourself in the face of future adversity?

Imagine a four-year-old version of yourself telling an older version of you that they made a mistake and feel sad. Speak aloud what you would tell them. Notice the tone of voice and words you are using, and think about what it would be like if you talked to yourself with the same tenderness and compassion.

Sometimes rejection is protection from what you thought you desired but may not have been the ideal fit. Think about something you really wanted that didn't work out. Were there positive things that later came through for you as a result of one door closing?

SHINE BRIGHTLY WITHOUT BURNING OUT

Do you ever feel like there are not enough hours in the day to get everything done? If so, it's time to take stock of your priorities and determine how to make the most of the time you have. In our fast-paced, performance-driven culture, there's pressure to fill every moment of our day in the pursuit of success. Throughout our lives, from the classroom to the sports field, we're often taught to place more value on our accomplishments, than developing who we are and focusing on our wellbeing.

Growing up, I often felt spread thin after a week overflowing with schoolwork, ballet classes, gymnastics practice, music lessons, Girl Scouts, swimming and several other projects. Although I enjoyed doing so many different things, I wish I could have spent more time relaxing and rejuvenating, and focusing on the interests and activities that inspired me the most.

While being our best self is an important part of growing as a person, it's important to remember that our inborn worth is not measured by the work we do, or the accolades we get. When we start with a baseline understanding that we are – and always will be – enough, it's easier to protect our energy, use our time mindfully and make decisions that help us thrive instead of breaking down.

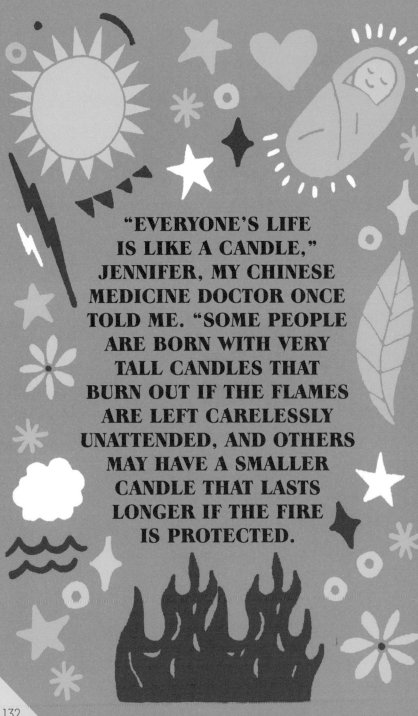

"EVERYONE'S LIFE IS LIKE A CANDLE," JENNIFER, MY CHINESE MEDICINE DOCTOR ONCE TOLD ME. "SOME PEOPLE ARE BORN WITH VERY TALL CANDLES THAT BURN OUT IF THE FLAMES ARE LEFT CARELESSLY UNATTENDED, AND OTHERS MAY HAVE A SMALLER CANDLE THAT LASTS LONGER IF THE FIRE IS PROTECTED.

YOU MAY HAVE A
SMALLER CANDLE
BECAUSE OF YOUR
ALLERGIES AND
CHRONIC ILLNESSES,

BUT HOW YOU
DEFEND AND
HONOUR YOUR
LIGHT IS UP
TO YOU."

STEP INTO YOUR POWER

SEE THE MENTAL AND PHYSICAL SIGNS OF BURNOUT CREEPING UP? HERE'S HOW TO COURSE-CORRECT.

* Know the signs. Changes in sleep patterns, appetite, energy level, mood and fatigue may indicate that you need to pause, reflect on what matters most to you, and take time to restore. If you notice these symptoms in yourself or a friend, talk to a trustworthy adult about getting support and resources.

* Be you. Some people gain energy by being around a lot of people, or filling their days with lots of hands-on engagement, while others need time alone to reflect, restore, and replenish their energy. It's perfectly normal to be either an introvert, an extrovert or anything in between – but it's important to know what you need to be your truest and brightest self.

* Honour your time. Write down your schedule for each week in a planner or on a blank piece of paper. Assign one hour per day as 'me time' that is reserved for something that nourishes you or gives you joy. It's up to you how you use your hour, but I suggest honouring your free time by making it a device-free, peaceful time where you're writing, resting, exercising, walking or creating art.

* Speak up. You have nothing to prove to anyone about your worth. I'm here to tell you that you belong. You are accepted, as you are. Anything else, is extra. There's no shame in not being perfect, asking for help, or needing support. Practise asking someone for help this week by kindly telling them what you need – without apology. If it helps, write them a note before you make your request in person.

DEALING WITH DIFFICULT TIMES

TRANSITIONS:
Read your way to presence
and a new perspective

LONELINESS

**HEALTHY
COMMUNICATIONS**

**COMMUNICATING
BOUNDARIES**

TRANSITIONS

"TOMORROW IS TOMORROW. FUTURE CARES HAVE FUTURE CURES, AND WE MUST MIND TODAY."
– Sophocles, *Antigone*

We often think we need to learn something new or do something more to heal discomfort, hurt and grief. I've found freedom, joy, growth and sometimes even discomfort in the awareness that the practice of unlearning what no longer serves or supports our healing is just as essential.

When I unpacked a dusty box of my old diaries, mixtapes (my generation's playlists) and scrapbooks during a recent trip to my childhood home, I reflected on my gratitude for the past and all the lessons I've learned along the way. I marvelled at each object as if it was new. These objects represented a realisation that helped me grow. Much of what I understood about the past evolved due to the

Read Your Way to Presence and a New Perspective

triumphs and hardships these pieces represented in material form. It turns out that just like me, my precious objects had been through a lot of highs and lows due to shifts that were often beyond their control and yet they, like me, were and are still here. They made it and they have meaning. I thought to myself, "I made it and I matter. As do my memories and what I do to evolve because of them."

Some items reminded me of my resilience as a human. I thought this as I read a note on the back of my ninth-grade graduation photo with an indiscernible facial rash that took multiple doctors a long time to solve. At the time, I railed when some well-meaning adults said, "this too shall pass," and dismissed my sadness and shame that I was the target of some rude playground jokes and would forever be enshrined in the yearbook with a face full of spots. And yet, despite the absolute validity of my

pain and my truth at that moment, I did eventually heal and grow. So much so that I now smile when I see that I showed up for that photo despite the almost unbearable anxiety I felt that day. I somehow got myself out of the bed and hopped onto the school bus after begging and pleading to my mum to let me call in sick. "I understand and want to hear how you feel, but it doesn't mean that these painful feelings or fears are more powerful than you are. Are you going to let some little spots take away your power or are you going to learn that the only way out is through? Now, keep

◉ STEP INTO YOUR POWER

CHANGE IS THE ONLY CONSTANT, AND YET IT IS OFTEN HARD. ARE YOU GOING THROUGH A TRANSITION? HERE ARE SOME ACTIVITIES I USE TO HELP ME COPE:

* **Create!** United States Poet Laureate Joy Harjo said, "What often follows periods of decay and destruction and chaos is rebuilding and renaissance – periods of fresh invention in thought and art. That's what often emerges from the ruins. You see little plants like after a fire... coming up from the char." Reflect on these words, read them aloud and close your eyes. What do you believe is the role of creativity, expression and art in times of crisis in your life? What would you like to see emerge from a challenge or obstacle you're processing, and how might writing, music or another way of expressing your creativity help you release and transform?

your head up and keep it moving." She advised me to read books about others who went through adversity and moved through it so that I would know that I wasn't alone.

Because of her advice, I was able to forgive myself for feeling ashamed of the range of painful emotions that came with the rash. I have since learned to pay attention to the little things and that includes the teachings we've observed directly and indirectly from people who care for and support us.

* **Book it**. After my mother passed away, I began to read her loving notes and inspiring thoughts in the pages of books she had given to me. Although I'm sad that she isn't physically here, I revisit her lessons and find new insights in the books she chose with intention throughout the stages of my life. My experience is that we don't move on, but we do move forwards after hard things happen. I'm still grieving, and I always will be, but I have a new relationship to the loss. Through these notes, I learned about her, and the ideas, passions and inspiration she sought to share with me. Think of someone you care about deeply and a book that you might want to share with them. Draw a picture of the book and write a note you might leave for them on the front page. What has the text you have chosen taught you about being present with your struggles, addressing them and moving forwards?

LONELINESS

What assumptions do people tend to make about you? How do they make you feel? For me, I can recall the annoying frequency of being typecast as both being self-interested and perpetually 'lonely' as an only or single child. Frankly, being perceived and labelled as being isolated, forlorn or distant caused me to feel the ache of loneliness more than the solitary nature of being my parents' only child ever did.

Although I delighted in the love and care I received from my parents, I was raised to make sure that the widespread stereotype about single children wasn't true. Sometimes I overextended myself and devoted too much energy in trying to prove this. I documented what I saw and heard to heal the tender void of feeling outside of the circle.

If I could create words, songs, poems, or drawings, then I knew that the world that I had within would be a friend and comfort no matter what. For me, my imagination and self-expression through creativity was the bridge I needed to make bonds with others outside of our home.

Behind the outgoing and confident exterior layer of myself was an occasionally shy and nervous introvert who felt like a misfit for being an only child. I soothed feelings of aloneness by writing myself into existence on my own terms and taking a sense of ownership about the differences that sometimes made me feel apart from others, even in the most crowded rooms. I realised that loneliness was a part of the path of my life, but not the entirety of its definition.

143

Sometimes I was the only single child, other times, I was the only new kid, the only Black girl; in some other cases, I was the only kid with a disability, the only girl in the brass section of the band, the only American, the only expat student when I returned to the states, the only kid who didn't yet speak or understand our new community's language and the only fill-in-the-blank in many spaces and places. For me, loneliness could be literal in terms of missing connection and meaningful contact with others, but often it felt like a struggle to belong in places where I found myself colouring outside of the lines even when I tried hard to play by the so-called rules. There is no shame in feeling lonely. Loneliness is like every other human experience in that there is no one way to experience it, heal it, or address it, but one thing is true, we don't have to bear it alone.

Whether your loneliness is due to a big transition in your life, family changes, being othered, grief, illness, social distancing, being distant from your loved ones, friend break ups, a feeling of being left out, rejected or left behind, or everything else in between, you are not alone, and help is available.

If you're feeling disconnection (whether it is with other people present or without) and you need support visit www.crisistextline.org wherever you are in the world to talk with someone.

STEP INTO YOUR POWER

Learn about how to address loneliness when it knocks on your door. Here are some activities you might find helpful:

* Express yourself

Take a moment to release what you're feeling. Sometimes loneliness is confusing and hard for us to understand or speak up about. Write down what you are feeling and trust the way it comes out. You could even try writing a haiku, drawing a picture, making a list or leaving yourself a voice memo about what is coming up for you.

* Write to someone who has passed on

I write letters to my late mother whenever I miss her. One of my friends writes letters to her favourite deceased artist who she imagined would have been her best friend. Read *The Diary of Anne Frank* to see the enduring power of letters to a friend during extraordinary crisis and loneliness.

* Be the change and help someone

"Learning to stand in somebody else's shoes, to see through their eyes, that's how peace begins. And it's up to you to make that happen. Empathy is a quality of character that can change the world." – Barack Obama.

Pay it forwards and reach out to someone else in need. Although grief is complex and not something we can 'fix', the ability to be a kind and generous force in other people's lives makes me feel less helpless and more empowered

* Connect with your crew

We live in an exciting time where there are virtual and in-person groups for just about every idea, interest or hobby. Take an opportunity to make new connections with likeminded people in safe and parent/guardian approved way by exploring a new activity. Whether you like languages, music, dance, gaming, reading, writing, sports or more, there are accessible virtual ways to learn something new and gain a new perspective.

HEALTHY COMMUNICATIONS

Have you ever found yourself saying 'yes' to keep the peace instead of staying true to your own needs and feelings? How did it feel in your body? Did you feel seen, cared for and heard? Now, envision yourself saying with a clear and honest voice what you emotionally and physically need to thrive.

My family raised me to be a curious and compassionate child, but sometimes my upbringing and empathic spirit led me to be an A+ people pleaser and conflict avoider. Despite my desire to read about independent and outspoken girls in books, I often absorbed both intentional and unconscious messages about automatic deference from my school, family, southern American culture, church and beloved sitcoms. Also, I sometimes experienced pushback or accusations of being 'too much' when I spoke my mind. I realised that being perceived as an agreeable and 'easy-going' girl was sometimes prioritised and rewarded over telling the truth.

Where did I learn to feel guilty about talking about my real feelings and needs? We live in a culture where we're too regularly taught to always respond with 'fine' or 'great' when asked how we are. Instead of sharing if we need support, or if we even have the capacity to fulfil a request, we're encouraged to abide by the terms that

other people set, before taking stock of what we need or feel.

When I tried to recall my first experience of that dynamic, I remember being told off for 'rudely' refusing to hug an older male family friend who made me feel uncomfortable. In that moment, although I didn't want to consent to embracing someone I didn't know, I felt ashamed that I was perceived by his partner and some other adults as snobbish and naughty. Now, I am aware that I had every right to set limits about my body and my choices about who to bring close and who to keep my distance from. In fact, I know it is compassionate, clear and honest to let the people in my life know what I need to feel comfortable and safe, in order to build and foster trust between us. That's why I appreciate when others share their hopes, needs and growing edges with me in kind.

While communications and practices vary depending on our background and beliefs,

respect is a widely held virtue that we should extend to others and ourselves. 'Treat others how you want to be treated' is a principle that has many names and manifestations in a variety of languages, traditions and approaches to life. Since I am aware that our communications style and strength is evolving and always able to be improved with time and practice, I challenge myself to stay kind, curious and consistent about fostering healthy communications.

STEP INTO YOUR POWER

* Ask open-ended questions. This allows us to deeply listen and show genuine interest in someone else's point of view. Practise asking questions that ask why/what/how/tell me more/what do you think about... Do this instead of leading or closed questions that may be unintentionally biased or based on assumptions. Think about the difference between telling your friend, "You're moving?! Aren't you worried about moving to a new school before the semester?" and "I heard your family is moving. How do you feel about changing schools?" Write down two leading questions and rephrase them as open-ended questions.

* Consider the context. If you need to have difficult or courageous conversation, consider asking the other party to speak in person or on a video call instead of texting. As humans, we also communicate through our body language and it is helpful to see and respond to others' cues. This helps us build trust and express empathy during sensitive moments.

* Use 'I' statements. Be as clear and direct as possible when you speak with others. Instead of saying, "You made me sad" consider saying "I feel sad when you yell at me". Modelling this style of communication moves us away from

assuming full intent and opens the door to allow others to own their actions and statements without shame or blame.

* **Be mindful of your body language.** Studies show that humans place a lot of focus on nonverbal communication, body language and tone of voice instead of the literal words when we're talking to someone. Since many cultures attach different meanings to eye contact, specific gestures, postures and movements, it is helpful to listen, observe and stay curious about what nonverbal messages you're giving and receiving within a specific context. For example, for some cultures, a thumbs up is a positive gesture and in others it is considered offensive.

* **Script it up.** Write a mini script about an interaction you had with someone where you wish you could re-author the narrative? What would it look like for you to reset the dynamic between you to include more open and respectful communication?

* **Viva la resistance.** Have you ever felt the urge to personalise someone else's unkind reaction or feedback after you expressed your truth? What if you embraced that their behaviour had everything to do with them, and nothing to do with you? What are some affirmations you might say to yourself to step into your power despite potential pushback? For example, "I define who I am. I am enough. Their words are theirs and not mine to own".

COMMUNICATING BOUNDARIES

Throughout my life, I have reimagined and replayed many instances where I wished I said no but chose a half-hearted or fear-driven yes to avoid conflict or loneliness. But when I think of the experiences that helped me grow, made me feel firm in my backbone and purpose and helped me expand my sense of personal integrity, I know that learning to express my limits was actually a way of expressing my freedom.

Some people are experts at respectfully setting boundaries. Others might struggle and feel that it is easier to deny their feelings because they fear being left out, disliked, invalidated or punished for genuine emotions, feelings or experiences. When I first started setting boundaries, I noticed some people in my life pushing back or making insensitive comments. Over time, I began to understand that many people who haven't been taught to respect their boundaries may feel uncomfortable when they see you claiming your personal power. But it is not your problem if they can't understand that your kind and well-defined statement of what respect looks, sounds and feels like is a thoughtful act and an investment in healthy communication. No matter how others perceive your boundary-setting, remember that considerately identifying and voicing your terms and limits is powerful and essential to our growth.

BOUNDARIES PROTECT US AND KEEP US SAFE.

151

Boundaries help release us from potential future resentment. Every time we set a respectful boundary that honours and expresses what we need to feel emotionally and physically safe in any situation, we open the door to modelling and fostering more integrity and resilience. Even though it can be tough to face our fears of being rejected or criticised, beautiful boundaries enable us to nourish ourselves instead of feeling depleted, burnt out or trespassed upon. Most of all, establishing our boundaries enables us to show others that we love them enough to show and tell them what we need to be free, because we want them to feel free too.

STEP INTO YOUR POWER

* Create a checklist

Healthy relationships are shaped by honesty, deep listening, openness, clear boundaries and respect for each other's feelings beyond our differences. Like any important skill, we improve our interactions with each other every time we engage with intention and compassion. Take a moment and visualise the kind of healthy communication you want to have more of in your life. Whether the communication you're thinking of is inspired by your own life or someone who motivates you, what aspects do you want to see more of in your relationships? Make a list so you can reference it before your next outing with a good friend. Here is what I have on my list:

· Be clear, compassionate and consistent.

· Ask how they prefer to be communicated with. Model by clearly and honestly expressing your own preferences: I prefer text and email to set up calls and video chats at another time. I like to plan my calls versus receiving spontaneous phone calls. It helps me stay focused and present.

· Be authentic and open-hearted. Be kind but be firm.

· Use 'I' statements. Listen. Try not to project.

· Be curious and ask questions.

· Don't overexplain.
'No' is a complete sentence.

· Ask to end the call if it is escalating to an unhealthy place. No yelling.

· Respond vs. React.

· Own your mistakes and apologise. Don't be defensive.

· Be true to your physical needs. Ask for what you need to feel safe and comfortable.

* Protect your energy

Do you have boundaries you'd like to set that focus on how others respect your support, time or energy?

* Hold yourself accountable

Do you keep boundaries with yourself? If not, be kind to yourself, and keep moving forwards. Every day provides us with an opportunity to start again when we have a setback. What is a boundary you will keep with yourself today? For example, I let my loved ones know that I need uninterrupted writing time each day in advance. My quiet time is sacred and when others see how seriously I take it, they usually follow suit.

* Don't be lost for words

Sometimes in the moment it can be hard to stay true to your boundaries and stick to what will serve you best. Jot down five boundary statements to keep with you to remind you that you will never be lost for words when you need them. Here are some of the concise phrases I keep close when I need them.

o Thanks for your input but I am clear about my decision.

o I hear you but I am sticking to my plan.

o No.

o I said no. No is my final answer.

o I don't feel comfortable with this direction/ decision/conversation/treatment/dynamic/ tone.

o I hear you but I am not OK with how you are speaking to/treating me. I am removing myself from this discussion.

o I don't feel safe in this conversation/ engagement/relationship.

o I need to take some time and distance. I'll let you know when and if I'm ready to restart this conversation.

o If this continues, I will stop this conversation.

o If you can't respect my boundary, I do not feel comfortable participating.

INDEX

FURTHER READING

Seeking further inspiration? Consider these resources as you continue to step into your power:

Books

Dear Ijeawele, or A Feminist Manifesto in Fifteen Suggestions,
by Chimamanda Ngozi Adichie

This Book Will Help You Change the World,
by Sue Turton

Little Leaders: Bold Women in Black History,
by Vashti Harrison

The Good Immigrant,
by Nikesh Shukla

Slay in your Lane,
by Yomi Adegoke

Girl Up,
by Laura Bates

Brit(ish),
by Afua Hirsch

You Have the Right to Remain Fat,
by Virgie Tovar

The Girl Guide,
by Marawa Ibrahim

Dare to Be Kind: How Extraordinary Compassion Can Transform Our World,
by Lizzie Velasquez

#NotYourPrincess,
by Lisa Charleyboy

Rookie Yearbook Three,
by Tavi Gevinson

I Am Malala,
by Malala Yousafzai

Demystifying Disability,
by Emily Ladau

Quiet Power,
by Susan Cain

This Book Is Feminist,
by Jamia Wilson

A Bigger Picture,
by Vanessa Nakate

Girls Resist,
by KaeLyn Rich

The Power Book, by
Claire Saunders, Georgia
Amson-Bradshaw, Minna
Salami, Mik Scarlet and
Hazel Songhurst

Online Resources

Crisis Text Line offers free
round-the-clock support
to all people experiencing
any kind of crisis via text.
https://crisistextline.org/

Teen Life offers non-
judgemental adult-
supervised peer-to-peer
support and resources.
https://www.teenline.org/

Mindfulness for Teens
offers free guided
meditations, app
access, and book
recommendations to help

you thrive and manage
stress. https://www.
mindfulnessforteens.com/

Peer Health Exchange
educates young people
about healthy decision-
making. https://www.
peerhealthexchange.org/
resources

Films

Own The Room

Maiden Trip

He Named Me Malala

Wadjda

If You Build it

I Am Greta

John Lewis: Good Trouble

Bully

Girl Rising

Step into My Power © 2022 Quarto Publishing plc. Text © 2022 Jamia Wilson. Illustrations © 2022 Andrea Pippins.

First published in 2022 by Wide Eyed Editions,
an imprint of The Quarto Group.
The Old Brewery, 6 Blundell Street, London N7 9BH, UK.
T (0)20 7700 6700 **www.Quarto.com**

ISBN 978-0-7112-7647-5

The illustrations were created digitally
Set in Futura and Grouch BT

Published by Georgia Amson-Bradshaw
Designed by Karissa Santos and Vanessa Lovegrove
Edited by Claire Grace and Katy Flint
Production by Dawn Cameron

Manufactured in Guangdong, China TT052022

9 8 7 6 5 4 3 2 1